Jody Tyler The Bull in the China Shop

Alex Mitchell

Published by Alex Mitchell, 2024.

JODY TYLER THE BULL IN THE CHINA SHOP

First edition. November 26, 2024.

Copyright © 2024 Alex Mitchell.

ISBN: 979-8891980327

Written by Alex Mitchell.

Also by Alex Mitchell

Table of Contents

Chapter One: The Path at Crabtree Cut-Off

In a late evening in spring, Dela Futrell sauntered down what is referred to as the Crabtree Cut-Off. The history of the State of Mississippi extends back thousands of years. The first recorded occupants are what is referred to as the Native American or Indigenous people. When the Europeans made their way to Mississippi, the Spanish would lay claim to the land. The Spanish would relinquish control of the land to the French and the British while pushing the Choctaw and the Chickasaw out. However, Dela's path on this 2024 evening had no Choctaw, Spanish, or French name because it had only been added in recent years. The Crabtree Cut-Off was a path a farmer had made to create a shortcut to the main highway from Eager Bend.

Eager Bend was a small group of run-down houses, if referred to as shacks, were doing the domiciles a modicum of flattery. This is where Dela lived with her aunt and uncle; Dela carried a bottle of cheap whisky as an offering to her aunt and uncle. They were drunks. Dela had earned the money by providing sexual favors for truck drivers near the highway weigh station. Dela found the men she serviced often rude and frequently smelly but still more likable than her aunt and uncle. Dela's aunt and uncle treated her meanly because Dela was deaf and mute. So many people made fun of her or treated her like she was stupid because they thought she had no idea what they were saying, but Dela could read their lips. Dela also had a plan. She was saving her money, and she had a favorite hiding spot. Soon, she would have enough money to leave her aunt and uncle to fin for themselves. She would go somewhere where people treated a deaf girl the same as anyone else.

THE EVENING LIGHT HAD started to dim as Dela walked. Both sides of the path were covered in tall brush and trees, but Dela saw a light coming down the path. Dela thought for a split second I could make more money. The thought was replaced with the fear that, in the remoteness, someone could take the money she had already earned. Dela is a thin-framed woman of twenty-two who looks more like a teenager than a young black woman. She had tomboyish features and short matter natural hair. Dela hid behind a tree to watch the pickup truck that had produced the light that startled her. She could see the driver as he passed. It was Darius Youngblood, a popular guy in these parts. But there was something wrong. The pickup he was driving belonged to someone else, and she knew it because she had been in the truck before. Darius was focused and did not look to either side of the path; he could not see her.

Dela resumed walking, but a serious of strange things happened. First, there was a big flash of high. The light was followed by a wave of force like wind directed and quickly radiated like the ripples from a pond. The force and the light had come from the shacks in at Edgar Bend. Dela took off running as fast as she could. Something was happening, and she had to know what it was. It did not take long for Dela to see what was wrong. One of the houses was ripped apart. The windows and doors had been blown off, and a massive hole was in the roof. Dela stood afraid to get too close to the destruction. A car drove up, and two men got out. They lit something and threw it into the devastation, and in seconds, the rubble was now entirely in a blaze. Before Dela could command her legs to run, an invisible force punched her in the chest. It catapulted her backward, landing her on her butt. It was a second explosion, most likely caused by the fire and the propane tank on the house. People started running out of their homes to see what was happening. Dela looked around, but the men starting the fire were gone. She sat on the ground, watching the blaze of the fire dance.

Chapter: Two The New Partner

"Alright, ladies, it is getting dark time for you all to go home," Jody commanded her softball team. The Team was comprised of young girls between the ages of fifteen and seventeen who had encountered run-ins with the law. Jody Tyler is five feet nine inches and built like a female weightlifter or ultimate fighter. Jody was assigned to train and work with the girls with Wendy's help. Wendy is the parole officer assigned to the girls of the softball team, who call themselves the Mississippi Bobcats.

"You're not worried about us being mistreated in the dark, boss?" Robbie, the girl assigned to play first base on the Team, taunted.

"Hell no. You girls are what makes the night dangerous. The sooner you take your butts home, the sooner the rest of the world will be safe."

The group chuckled at Jody's assessment. Many girls were being picked up by parents or relatives who had come to watch the practice. The parents who were there to watch over the young female paroles were often referred to by the group as Mama Bears. Some girls lived too far away or had no one to give them a ride, so they were shuttled in the county van Wendy drove.

Jody noticed a man walking across the field, heading for the group. His eyes were fixed on her.

"Alright, boss, I see why you are in such a hurry to get rid of us. You have a date." Kayla, the shortstop, commented.

"He aint my date."

"Then can I have him?" Kayla shot back.

"Alright, you thug, you and anyone that laughed at that owes me twenty push-ups at the start of the next practice." Jody saw a look of almost recognition in the gaze of the man approaching. He wore a blue suit that was too nice to have come from any nearby store. The man wore expensive shoes that were no match for the Mississippi mud of the Gangler High School ballfield where the Bobcats practiced. The approaching man had a serious look accented by a slight scar on his lip. This man was strong and tough, but not just for appearance's sake; he had been in his fair share of fights.

"Hand me my backpack from beneath the seat." Jody requested of Wendy. Without a word, Wendy reached into the van. She retrieved the backpack in a maneuver that only a preplanned exchange could offer. The remaining teenage ball team members got hurriedly into the van, sensing something about to transpire. Jody unzipped the backpack and slipped her hand into the pack slowly.

"No need for the cannon, Detective Tyler." The approaching man called out before Jody could retrieve her weapon. "My name is Detective Vaughn, and I am your new partner." Detective Vaughn slowly pushed back his suit jacket and revealed his badge.

"I am Wendy. I am like the den mother to this mob of would-be criminals." Wendy pushed past Jody, who still seemed not to have decided to remove her service weapon.

"Detective Wade Vaughn." Detective Vaughn accepted Wendy's handshake.

"Wendy Coltrane, Department of Parole and Probation." Wendy was a thin black woman with thick glasses and a built-in smile. The type of smile that disarms anger issues frequently. Wendy wore braids, and even in casual clothing, she looked like she should be teaching social studies at the local high school. All Wendy charges adore Wendy if not for her somewhat out-of-place look and demeanor but for having heard stories from others on parole or probation and how the personality of the convict and the parole officer could collide in the worst possible ways.

"But don't hold that against her. She is one of the good guys." One of the girls affirmed from the now loaded van.

With a stare of skepticism, Jody finally accepted the handshake from her new partner.

"We have a case. Lieutenant Singleton asked me to retrieve you." Detective Vaughn announced.

"Where did you park?" Jody asked.

"I was dropped off. I watched the last part of the practice. We will need to take your truck." With that, Detective Vaughn began walking toward Jody's truck.

"How exactly does he know which truck is yours and where you parked?" Wendy whispered in Jody's ear.

"I am still working on how he knew my .45 was in this backpack."

Chapter Three: Getting to Know You

Jody's nickname is Bull. Short for Bull in a China shop. As a child, she was clumsy and reckless. She loved to hang out with her brothers, and she performed in sports as well as any of them. Jody was the person who frequently would charge into a situation without fear or forethought. Now, sitting here in her Pickup truck, traveling to the destination provided by Detective Vaughn, was killing her. He seemed calm, with no conversation and a stranger inches away. Finally, she could stand it no more. "Where were you a detective before?"

"New York." Detective Vaughn answered quietly as he stared out the passenger window, watching the night invade the last remaining light.

"The city or the state?"

"The city."

"Then you will find this quite different."

"How." Detective Vaughn answered, trying to get a text on his cell phone.

"For one thing, many of the places you are going to have little or no cell reception," Jody answered, then glanced down at Detective Vaughn's shoes. "Do the Detectives in New York do a lot of dancing when they are on a case?"

"Very seldom." He murmured.

"Then those are the wrong shoes for anywhere I can think of here other than a dance hall."

"Understood."

"Mississippi is 48,430 square miles. From Hernando to Woodville and from Corinth to Pascagoula. Ever sweet mile of it is now your jurisdiction." Jody paused to be sure Detective Vaughn was paying attention. "What is the population of New York City?"

"Close to eight and a half million, give or take."

"The total population of Mississippi is just under 3 million. That means your city is more than double the population of the entire state of Mississippi. But not to worry. New York City is over double the population of at least 25 of the fifty states."

Jody now knew Detective Vaughn was listening to hear. "We do investigation, but we also provide support to local law enforcement, even if sometimes they don't think they need our help. We also back up and support federal agencies, especially when they are smart enough to let us know they need our help." Again, Jody paused. "Any questions?"

"Yes, now that you ask. What is the deal with you managing a girls' softball team?"

"A couple of the local judges thought there were some girls that were in trouble but not really bad apples. They felt that if the girl entered the regular judicial process, they would learn from the seasoned cons, and before you know it, they would be just as bad if not worse."

"No, I meant, why you?" Vaughn corrected.

"It was supposed to be a punishment. I slugged a highway patrol officer."

"Oh. I see."

"No, you don't see I was groped."

"Hardly seems fair. Did he get punished, too?"

"She."

"Oh. I See."

"Stop with the I see shit. A lot of people that go to the gym and take care of their bodies are gay. Sometimes people assume."

"So, if she grabbed you, why would you be punished?"

"We let it be written up as a cross-complaint. That way, no one's career is down the toilet. And the nasty buzzed that officers do would not have a chance to start."

"Are they any good? Your Team, I mean." Vaughn asked.

"My last Team went 45 and one. This Team has the potential to be even better."

"That is impressive."

"And thank you."

"For what?"

"Well, most of the time when I am picking up a guy that doesn't know me or what to expect, they stare at me the way a little kid stares at the next big ride in an amusement park."

"I have a lot on my mind and needed the information. Maybe I can ogle you later." Vaughn joked.

For a moment, Jody felt the warm comfort of having just met someone who needed her help. The horror supplanted this feeling she felt as they had reached their destination.

Chapter Four: The Sence of the Crime

A massive wave of fear and foreboding overcame Jody as she slammed the truck to a stop. As a police detective, Jody has been on her fair share of scenes where a tragedy occurred; however, this was different. Police cars, fire trucks, and the coroner truck surround the demolished remains of a shack that was once someone's home. Personal possessions had been sprue throughout the perimeter and if shot out of a cannon. The rickety frame of work of a burned-out carcass was what remained. Sherrif's deputies were interviewing people who had come from their homes to watch. Many spectators had been caught in various stages of dress or undress. All wanted answers more from the deputies than the deputies wanted from them. Still, it was not the hellacious nightmare scene that made Jody's blood run cold and sent her running toward the house, but it was the fact that she knew whose house it was. The house had belonged to Darius Youngblood's mother before her passing. Darius has kept the house and often used it as a place to have extramarital affairs. Of this, Jody was sure because she had been one of the guests participating in sex with Darius. Fear, Confusion, and humiliation collided like three runaway freight trains and now collided on a track right before her.

The smell of stale, rotted, and moldy wood mixed with the scent of death.

"Slow down." A fireman yelled as he blocked Jody from charging up to the structure.

Jody shook her head to clear the fog. The fireman was Bobby Joe Tyler, her brother.

"I got her." It came from Detective Vaughn, who had raced to catch up with Jody.

"No. I got her." Boddy Joe shot an angry look at Vaughn. "Lieutenant Singleton is here, and she wants to talk to the both of you."

"WELL, NICE OF YOU TWO to join us." Lieutenant Cara Singleton announced, and she stepped from a gathering of investigators. Lieutenant Singleton was 5 foot 5 and slightly stocky with scrubbed skin. She wore a business suit with a shoulder holster that reviewed the butt end of a gun that would seem too large for her to find useful.

"Was he in there?" Jody finally formed the question.

"My questions first, Detective." Singleton seemed to be getting a perverse pleasure from controlling the information Jody needed. "First question is for Detective Vaughn." After shaking it, Lieutenant Singleton took Detective Vaughn's hand and held it momentarily. Singleton visually surveyed Vaughn, and her gaze showed she approved her assessment. "Detective Vaughn, it's good to finally meet you in person. Did you do what you were ordered to do?"

A mix of nervousness and embarrassment appeared on Detective Vaughn's face. "Yes."

Jody stared at Detective Vaughn, wondering what had been concealed from her.

"I checked the hoods of her truck and the van. Neither had been driven recently upon my arrival," Detective Vaughn answered fully.

"You're an asshole." Jody shot at Detective Vaughn.

"Not at all. He was quite reluctant to do it, but it was a direct order from a superior. You remember direct orders from superiors, don't you, Detective Tyler? Not everyone has a well-connected father to cover their ass."

Jody and Detective Vaughn stared at each other like two petulant children who had just been separated from fighting over the last piece of candy.

"Next, your question Detective Tyler. And I apologize if it stings, but have you been sexually active with Darius Youngblood in the last year to year and a half?"

"She doesn't have to answer that." Jody had not even noticed Bobby Joe was still standing there.

"No. We broke it off longer than that," Jody answered while trying to read the frustration mounting on her older brother's face. She loved Bobby Joe and all her brothers; her sin had already caused them shame. She wonders how much more of her past mistakes would injure her family.

"Why is that important?" Detective Vaughn asked.

"Because your new partner was sleeping with the man who may have just been blown up in his house. And because that means I have firemen, State Cops, Local Cops, and federal people who want answers. So, before I let your partner anywhere near this case, I want to know she is not in the middle of it."

Lieutenant Singleton's comment made Jody stare, but she could not produce words that would help the ugly unfolding of her past poor judgment.

"Since your brother decided to abandon the great state of Mississippi, I hope Detective Vaughn can help with some mental heavy lifting around here."

A heavy-set patrolman walked up to the group and stated. "Some of the people questioned say that woman there was here first. She is Dela."

"Then why don't we ask her what she saw?" Detective Vaughn asked.

"Because she is Dela the Dummy. She can't hear or speak." The Patrolman answered.

Slowly, Detective Vaughn walked over to Dela, who was still sitting on the ground, holding the bottle of whiskey like an infant.

"Hello Dela, my name is Detective Vaughn." Slowing, Vaughn introduced himself.

"I told you she is a dummy, and she can't hear you," the Patrolman reiterated.

"Patrolman, the only one who is a dummy is your father for lying down with your mother and coming up with you," Vaughn said.

"Why I don't have to take that kind of shit from some sissy shoe-wearing..."

"Relax, patrolman, it was just a test," Vaughn informed.

"I don't see what gives M.B.I. the balls to test a veteran officer," the Patrolman yelled.

"The test wasn't for you. It was for Dela."

"What?" Jody asked, not to clarify what she was witnessing.

"When I commented, I never took my eyes off her. But her eyes shifted to the right to see how you would respond even before you spoke."

"It is not a magic act. She can read lips. And you guys were about to miss that." Lieutenant Singleton explained.

"So, question her," Jody suggested.

"No. Because if we get a suspect and send them to trial. Some lawyers could argue that she never knew exactly what she was asked. Those same lawyers could throw out any information we collect based on anything she might give us." Vaughn explained. We get someone from family services or some other expert to help us interview her.

"Like I said, he is here to do the mental heavy lifting for your partnership, Tyler." Singleton started to walk away, then stopped and turned back around. "And to answer your question, there were two bodies. We suspect one male and one female. Look at the bright side: They probably came right about when the window blew out and never knew they went."

Chapter Five: A Long Ride Home

Detectives Tyler and Vaughn fidgeted for a while, once alone on the drive from the explosion scene. The two detectives had spent time securing information that had been collected before their arrival and made plans to assist in keeping all involved agencies apprised of the progress of the investigation. At first, it was clear that Jody was lost in her thoughts as the memories of what Darius had meant to her flashed through her mind like an uncensored and unrestrained newsreel.

Vaughn was unhappy with the intermittent cell service. Still, he did not want to complain aloud as he knew Jody was sitting beside him, wrestling with her own demons.

"I apologize for calling you an asshole." Finally, Jody spoke.

"How do you know I'm not?"

"I guess I don't. But I apologize for screaming it in your face. That was unprofessional."

"So let me ask a couple of questions on my mind, and maybe you will find out if I am or not," Vaughn suggested.

"Shoot."

"How did your husband feel about Darius?"

"I don't have a husband," Jody answered.

"The big fireman, I think he is the battalion commander. He gave me a funny look when I reached for your arm. He was wearing a name tag that is the same last name as yours, and I happened to hear him whisper to you he cooked dinner, and it was in the refrigerator. So, me being a moderately good detective assumed...."

"That was Bobby Joe, my brother. We have been sharing a house that used to belong to an aunt of mine who passed away. Most of the time, he sleeps over at the fire station, and I am gone a lot, so it works out perfectly."

"I thought Lieutenant Singleton said your brother is a cop, and he left Mississippi."

"Now I see the problem. New York is so big that you are only allowed to have one sibling. Well, Mr. Moderately Good Detective, I have seven brothers and six sisters."

"Wow. What do your parents do besides the obvious answer."

"That's nasty, and I will ignore it; next real question."

"Singleton said you have pull. What the hell does that mean?" Vaughn asked.

"My father was chief of Police. He still has friends and contacts in various agencies."

"So, she is afraid you may take her job?" Vaughn guessed.

"Some women in positions of power, rather than supporting other women, see them as competition. Maybe that is why she was flirting with you."

"I didn't notice any flirting, but her game seems to be to divide and conquer."

"How so?"

"She could have just as easily had the Patrolman that dropped you off at the ballfield check your car and report back. She wanted us to clash."

"That sneaky back-biting son of a bitch."

"Last question. Did you kill Darius or have him killed?"

"No." The weak tremor of Jody's voice betrayed her, and her feelings for Darius showed.

"So, I suggest we let the local police question and interview anyone connected with you who might be seen as having a motive to set fire to Mr. Youngblood, and we concentrate on everything else."

"You are taking my word that I had nothing to do with it?"

"Sure. Why not?"

"Then I take back what I said about you being an asshole."

Chapter Six: Knowing Only What Must Be Know About Those Around Us

Jody had suffered a restless night. She had been constantly awakened by dreams of her romantic encounters with Darius, replaced with darker dreams. Jody's dark dreams were first the dreams of what her brothers had done to humiliate Darius when they were all younger. The darkest dream, however, was of Darius trapped in his mother's old house, engulfed by flames, and calling for her to rescue him.

Jody had chosen to continue working from the Lamont Police Station. Her father had been chief at this station before retiring and becoming a writer. Jody felt comfortable with most of the officers and staff and felt any outside agency looking for her to add information would be able to locate her there. She was slightly surprised that Detective Vaughn was already at work when she arrived. When Jody reached the desk Detective Vaughn had appropriated, he reached over, located a large box of donuts, opened it, and showed the contents to Jody like a peace offering. Jody dropped a pair of men's boots she was carrying at Vaughn's feet.

"Put these on." She commanded.

"Yes, ma'am. These are filled with lemon, raspberry, and some with cream. I am sorry, but they were out of any filled with wheatgerm or grass clippings, or however, you usually take yours."

Jody could not help but smile. "Are we still a little singed by my poor behavior yesterday?" Jody accepted a donut and ate while Vaughn changed shoes.

"The local examiner is sure he has the charred remains of two bodies, one male and one female. He will let us know when he has more. We were able to contact Family Services, and they will send someone over to visit Dela. We need to visit where she stays to get a good feel for what information we can get from her."

Jody could spend the next couple of hours bringing Vaughn up to speed on the case she was involved with and how their help was expected. Immediately, Jody noticed that Detective Vaughn was brilliant and caught on quickly. In Detective Vaughn's feedback, Jody noticed that in his past experiences as a big city detective, he could offer alternative choices to investigating and problem-solving. However, Jody also noticed that something was missing from Vaughn's conversations. He made no mention of friends or family. Jody started to wonder if he was deliberately omitting anything about his personal connections or if it was something of a regional difference in how he communicated.

Jody also began to wonder if Detective Vaughn was mentally preparing himself for the fact that she may have in some way been involved in the death of two people.

"Well, enough of this office work, let's say we go do some face-to-face police work. We can start the Futrell's, Dela's folks that should give us a warm-up for the tough stuff." Jody usually wore jeans and one of her sports coats. As Jody stood, she began checking her service weapon and noticed that Detective Vaughn was staring at her. "It's a competition-type model 1911 45. My father gave it to me when he retired the bone grip was his idea."

"Seems a little excessive for what we do," Vaughn observed.

"My father always says better the devil, you know."

Chapter Seven: And in New York

"I'm glad you're back." Viola Barrington-Vaughn stated in an unmasked, insincere tone. Viola Barrington-Vaughn was one of three Baxter-Caldwell Holding Inc. vice presidents. Her stepsister and stepbrother were the other two vice presidents. Viola sat behind the massive marble-topped desk of a former dictator that she had flown in from the country that had collapsed around him. The desk had ivory and gold handles on the drawers. There was black oak wood that framed the desk. There were several dark stains in some areas of the legs of the desk. She knew the stains were blood stains from the previous owner.

"How was your flight?"

"Too long. Too dirty and other than that shitty in general." Marcus Newport, or so he now called himself, answered. Marcus Newport had worked for the Barrington family for over thirty years. He was in his mid-sixties and had served in the military with Viola's father. Marcus wore a tailored suit and sat facing Viola in one of the visitors' chairs.

"How is my father?"

"Pissed off. But what's new."

"Are you sure that's the way you want to answer me?" A hint of impending disaster emitted from within Viola and shot through her eyes.

"Look, I have worked for your family my entire adult life. I literally owe my life to your father. But I will always be your protector, even when it means protecting you from yourself." Marcus confirmed his allegiance.

Viola swiveled her gold-trimmed calves leather chair around and faced the window behind her before continuing to assess the information she was collecting.

"How is he taking that fuck up in Boseman?" A recent F.B.I. raid had caused the destruction and confiscation of some materials that Baxter-Caldwell was due to ship overseas.

"He is livid about that, but he is blaming your brother..."

"Half-brother." Quickly, Viola corrected.

"He is ready to roast his chestnuts over an open flame."

"Bryce is a whore mongering idiot and a coke head but how the hell was he supposed to know the guy he thought helped produce the plan to redistribute wealth thought Europe had stolen the plan from his ghostwriter."

"Your father says Bryce had every chance to recheck his intel; instead, he was somewhere stoned under a pile of overweight hookers. He is putting together a plan to redistribute Bryce's duties. His first thought was to give some of the responsibility to your husband."

"Holly shit." Viola spun around in her chair.

"Do you mind if I have a drink?" Viola nodded, and Marcus walked to the bar in the room and made them both drinks.

"As much as I want my husband back in my bed, my father wants him back in this company."

"That is about how I see it. I plan to watch your husband, but it won't be easy."

"Why, where is he?"

"My sources say he is in Oktibbeha."

"What planet is that on?" Viola asked.

"It's in Mississippi."

"Please tell me that is a black joke. Is Mississippi still even a state?"

"I have a plan. I know a guy who knows a guy. Anyway, there is a female private investigator who comes from that area. We have her collect as much intelligence as possible before you decide. That way, you are not left standing there with your dick in your hand, so to speak, like your half-brother."

"Find this hillbilly investigator. Bring her in blind and let me interview her as soon as possible. When my father returns from China, I want as much of this squared away as possible."

Marcus had the instructions he needed to set up his operation, but Viola stopped him as he was preparing to leave.

"Marcus, if some country bitch has had her hands on my husband, be sure to let me know." Marcus smiled. Fieldwork always made him smile.

Chapter Eight: The House of Futrell

The houses in the Edger Bend area were scattered, with one in more ill repair than the next. In daylight, poverty's true despair and hopelessness were most prominent. Jody knew she was keeping things from Vaughn, but she hoped that things she knew would remain as the specters that haunted her and had little need to surface and infest the growing partnership.

"Hi, Dela." Vaughn waved as he and Jody were allowed into the Futrell home. The home was loaded with useless items and old clothing. It was as if the Futrell couple collected everything someone else discarded.

Blanch Futrell was a heavy woman with a fat, round face, and greasy skin that made her look like she was looking out through an aspect mold. She wore a loose-fitting moo moo of an undefined color and age. Stains had made their permanent impression on Blanche's garment, and they were there to stay.

Barney Futrell sat in an old chair that had permanently contoured to his fat ass. Barney Futrell sat watching a T.V. screen with some form of mindless rerun playing that made you wonder if anyone was foolish enough to consider this entertainment 20 years ago. The stench of the couple was powerful, and it was as if the couple was having a contest to see who could make your eyes water first.

Dela had been watching when Jody and Vaughn entered the home. She was on her hands and knees scrubbing the kitchen floor. Dela looked up at Vaughn, smiled, and waved.

"She needs to stop gawking at men folk and finish her chores. She knows she likes to wander out free at night, and she can't do that if she aint done her chores first."

Jody could feel that she was entering a part of the relationship between her and her new partner, and she could feel him getting upset or displeased with things, even if he did not express it. She was also hoping he could do the same where she was concerned.

"Ma'am, we are with the Mississippi Bureau of Investigation, and we had a couple of questions about what you can recall from last night." Jody began to get things focused.

"More cops. I swear, that got to be where all the tax dollars go. First, we get questioned by the sheriff and his idiot deputies; then, we get questions from the state troopers. Now, here you guys come to ask the same questions. Well, I will give you an answer that can go a long way. And you and all your cop pals can have a meeting and quote me on this. The fucking house just blew up. End of story." Barney ranted as if his rerun of a rerun was being interrupted.

"One or two explosions?" Vaughn asked, and he scribbled on a notepad.

"Two. I remember we heard the first one, and I went to grab a robe to be decent if I stepped outside. And no sooner than I found my robe than another boom came." Blanch filled in as she poured herself whiskey from the cheap whisky Dela had brought home.

"When was the last time you saw anyone over there?" Vaughn asked.

"The boys are always coming and going; no one keeps track," Barney said, getting his share of the whiskey.

"What, boys?" Jody asked.

"Well, lately, it's been Darius and Ricky. Sometimes, they entertain women. If you want to stretch it by calling it entertaining and if you want to stretch it further by referring to them as women." Blanch added in a bitter tone.

"I am new around here; who is Ricky?" Vaughn asked.

"Ricky Sells, if you stopped by the Cut-Rate gas station, you probably saw him there. He works the service counter and stocks. A skinny kid in his mid-twenties follows Darius around like Darius was the Messiah."

"What type of vehicle does Ricky drive?" Vaughn asked.

Jody could tell Vaughn had something on his mind.

"Black Chevy pickup, but I couldn't even guess the make or year," Barney answered.

"The extended cab Ford that burned up in the driveway was Darius's machine," Jody added.

"MIND IF WE STOP AT the Cut-Rate gas station on our way?" Jody asked Vaughn immediately after they were on their way.

Jody checked by phone as they drove. It was definitely a man and a woman that were burned to death. And the truck that burned was definitely registered to Darius.

Jody and Vaughn knew the trip to the Cute-Rite gas station was taking them out of their planned daily routine, but it was like collecting breadcrumbs, with one crumb more compelling than the next. Jody also knew this was an excellent time to show a City Detective what it is like to be able to cross into a different county, ask questions, and return without significant fanfare. Jody had also planned a meeting with Lieutenant Singleton to give a progress report and a meeting with Chickasaw County sheriffs and county officers regarding an issue she had been tracking. It was guaranteed to be a long day, and it was getting longer by the minute.

"Habib, what can you tell me about Ricky Sells, and where can I find him?" Jody asked the Clerk in the Cut-Rite. The Clerk was wearing a greasy smock with Habib on the name tag. He was a tall, thin twenty-something-year-old with long, stringy hair and tattooed arms and neck. The Clerk had long, thin fingers with yellow tips. The type of fingers no one wanted him to hand them anything. He had bulbous eyes with red veins in them that looked like he had not slept in days. Yet, the Cute-Rite clerk performed his duties like a combination of the employee of the month and a one-man band. He was stocking while ringing customers up as well as giving directions to drivers.

"My name aint no fucking Habib lady." The Clerk snapped. "Habib is probably in India practicing the Kamasutra, for all I know. He quit two days after taking this stinking job. My uniforms are all dirty because I wasn't even supposed to work today. Ricky ups and just doesn't show up to relieve me. I called my boss, and she said that means you have to work a double. I tell her no, Lady, that means you guess I have to work a triple because the poor sap relieving me this evening is me."

John, the Clerk, looked around like he was expecting someone to call him away, then continued. "My boss says don't forget to clean the restrooms at least three times per shift. Where in the world does it say a clerk's job is to clean toilets? It aint just the men's toilets that usually bad enough but if you ever clean a women's toilet that is something you will never forget. I have cleaned shit from the middle of the floor, and it was the cleanest and most sanitary thing in there, Lady."

"Detective Tyler. She worked hard for that title. If you could refer to her as Detective Tyler instead of Lady." Vaughn requested. "Does Ricky miss a lot of shifts?"

The Clerk looked at Vaughn as though he had to read and translate what was said before responding. By this time, it was time for the Clerk to ring out several inpatient customers.

"Turn your back. I'm going to smack him in the face." Jody whispered to Vaughn.

"You will do no such thing." Vaughn smiled.

"John. My name is John. And Ricky did not used to be absent or late. It wasn't until he started hanging out with King Ding Dong." John, the Clerk, informed them upon his return.

"Who?" Vaughn asked, stopping his notetaking.

"Some slick dude named Darius something or other. The chicks can't wait to drop their drawers for this guy. They stand in line having fist fights for his action."

Jody knew she was now getting upset, and it would eventually reflect badly on her if she could not control it. She took a step back so Detective Vaughn could ask questions.

"You guys' trade shifts and cover each other, so you have his number and address in your contacts on your phone, right," Vaughn affirmed.

John went to retrieve his cell phone.

"Look, we will talk about this later," Vaughn said in a tone meant to calm Jody.

"Yeah, that Darius guy gets all the ass. I don't mean just skanks and hoes. I mean, a normal, respectable, and stuck-up chick can't wait to get it on with his guy. He had been letting Ricky handle some of the overflow." John returns, muttering.

"Make him stop talking, or I swear to God I will," Jody whispered to Vaughn.

"Here is the address and number, but you might want to visit the hospital. Ricky's regular girlfriend is a nurse there. Maybe she knows where he is. Her name is Lena. She is ugly as the thing that ate my grandpa's dog, but she has a pleasant enough personality."

Jody looped her arm under Vaughn's and led him from the gas station.

JODY KNEW SHE WAS SULKING but felt she could not control it. This case was exposing her mistakes as a person, and the nicer Vaughn seemed to be about it, the more upset she became. The ride to the hospital had been quiet. John was correct about one thing about which Lena was concerned. She was personable and, therefore, easy to find. All the employees knew who she was. Her shift supervisor found Lena and suggested to Jody and Vaughn that they use her office for their discussion.

Lena's shift manager led her to the office and gave the detectives a look of concern as she departed the meeting.

"Why are you looking for Ricky?" where the first words Lena could speak. She was dressed in hospital whites. Lena was a simple-looking girl who was very pregnant. She had acne scarring on her face and an intense stare, and her accent was from the Delta or Louisiana.

"We are collecting information from any possible witnesses from a fire," Vaughn answered.

"You are Detectives. We deal with Police here all the time. Something else is going on." Lena sat in the office chair and rested her arm on her stomach. "It's that Goddamn Darius?"

"Ricky did not make it to work for his shift at the gas station. When was the last time you saw him?" Jody asked.

"Two days ago. He said they had a big deal working, and if it worked out, he would be able to leave the gas station. I told him I don't care if he cleans up behind horses as long as he comes home to me at night." A wave of emotion washed over Lena, and she was crying. "Is he dead?"

"Right now, all we know is that there was a fire, and we are trying to find out who was where when the fire occurred." Detective Vaughn oversimplified.

"Watch out for the Darius. He is bad news. Ricky would go out with him and come home smelling like some other woman's cologne. He said it was business, but what kind of business is that?"

JODY AND VAUGHN BARELY made it to the meeting on time. It was being held in one of the conference rooms in the Lamont Police station. Jody's brother and battalion commander, Bobby Joe Tyler, sat in for the arson investigator. Doctor Spearman from the medical examiner's office was in attendance. Lieutenant Singleton came to the meeting, but she did not like having it in the Lamont station and made sure everyone was aware of it.

Jody began with a recap of their investigation thus far.

"Sounds like your ex-flame was a busy boy?" Lieutenant Singleton sneered.

"Excuse me, but can we keep this short and as professional as possible? I have my own Team to work with. We certify C.P.R. for lifeguards this evening, so some parents don't lose a child in a public pool. I want to be there." Bobby Joe's commanding voice brought the room back to its intended purpose. Bobby Joe was tall and had a body like he worked out all his life. He had a handsome face and sharp eyes, the type of eyes that told you he was listen to your every word.

"I'm sorry; it's my fault this place gives me the creeps. Please begin your presentation," Lieutenant Singleton requested.

Bobby Joe walked to an easel and planted a picture on a poster board of a house. "The initial blast came from a device made from dynamite that was under the bed. Far more than what was needed for the job. It sent force through the roof of the house."

"What about the second blast?" Vaughn attempted to interrupt.

"Hold your horses; I am getting there. After the blast, firebombs were thrown through the windows."

"Jesus Christ," Jody exclaimed.

"The fire ignited compression in the propane tank, which was the second blast." Bobby Joe concluded, then turned to Dr. Spearman, letting him know the floor was now his.

"Well, you know how on T.V. someone can take a single ass hair and tell you whose ass out of the billions of asses in the world it came out of. Well, I aint that guy. And you know the expensive machines they have in New York. Well, I don't have any of those, and if I did, I doubt they would tell you either. But what I can tell you is that if you can give me something to match it against, I can tell you the percent of the likelihood that was one of the people in that explosion and firebombing."

"Detectives, it looks like the ball is back in your court." Singleton proclaimed.

JODY HAD TO SUPERVISE practice for her softball team, so she invited Vaughn to come to the practice to discuss future strategies. She also wanted him to be aware of the Chickasaw County issue they had been assigned. Vaughn agreed but asked if they could stop by the place where he was staying on the drive to the ballfield. Vaughn was staying in a boarding house run by Miss Addie. Miss Addie knew Jody, but Miss Addie was close to 100 years old, and her memory was starting to fail. Often, she confused Jody with one of her sisters and, at times, with Jody's mother when she was Jody's age.

Jody followed Vaughn down the second-floor corridor of the old boarding house. For a moment, she had a feeling of dread. What if this is a ploy to try and seduce me? Jody was concerned not because she did not think she could fight off his advances but because she wondered if she would. He had never mentioned a wife, but surely someone as put together as he had someone. And did he respect her? He had spent the day learning of her wilder exploits as a younger girl. Did he think she was a whore.

Chapter Nine: Enter Sabrina

Just as Vaughn reached for the door to his apartment, it opened. There stood Sabrina Vaughn, Detective Vaughn's daughter. Sabrina was a wiry 14-year-old girl with a long ponytail. She had huge brown eyes that were identical to her father's. Sabrina had a heartwarming simile.

"Oh, my, you are lovely. What is your name?" Jody asked.

Sabrina led them both into the room without a word. She wrapped herself around her father's waist and leaned against him. Vaughn playfully pushed back. It was like a child's game of tug-of-war. The game may have been coming to a point where Sabrina was getting too old to play it, but the joy it still brought her resonated in her face.

"This is Sabrina, my daughter. She is not being rude. She cannot speak or hear." Vaughn informed Jody.

"Oh, shit, that is why you were so mad about Dela."

Sabrina smiled and covered he mouth.

"What's so funny," Jody asked.

"She knows what you just said. She reads lips well."

Sabrina signed for her father.

"No, I said she is my partner," Vaughn answered and signed back to Sabrina.

Sabrina signed something else to her father.

"Okay. You guys are talking about me." Jody concluded.

"When I told her you were my partner, she asked if that meant you couldn't be my girlfriend, too," Vaughn answered, walking away to retrieve something from his bedroom.

"Let me know what you decide on that one," Jody mumbled, and Sabrina smiled and covered her mouth. I have and I deal, so why don't you join us? We are going to watch my girls play softball."

"I am in the process of getting a divorce. It has been challenging, to say the least. Since you have not yet asked, this little culprit keeps texting me when we are in areas with no signals. I have not yet found a school to take her, but I have some leads. So far, she has been spending her day reading and helping Miss Addie clean." Vaughn spoke as he returned from the bedroom. He had taken off his sports jacket and put on a casual jacket.

Chapter Ten: Sabrina Meet the Girls

"What are you in for, convict?" Gloria, the pitcher of the Mississippi Bobcats, called out as Sabrina, Jody, and Vaughn walled across the ballfield. The Team ran to meet the new team member.

"She is not a con. I am Detective Vaughn, and she is my daughter."

"Well, there is no reason she can't train with us as an unofficial team member." Wendy, the parole officer, suggested.

"If you want to be official, I know a liquor store we can hit." Rosie, the catcher, joked, and all the girls started laughing.

"That had better be a joke because I have locked up a lot of people like you," Vaughn commented.

"You mean Mexicans?"

"No young people with a sense of humor," Vaughn replied.

"What's your name?" Wendy asked.

"She can't speak or hear. Her name is Sabrina. "Jody answered.

"Out of site. You mean if someone calls you a bad name or if your mom tells you to scrub the toilet with a toothbrush, you don't even hear that crap." Gloria confirmed.

"All right, ladies' social hour is over. Let's get warmed up, including you, Miss Sabrina."

WHILE THE BOBCATS TRAINED, Jody and Vaughn sat and reviewed several other police issues that had to be addressed. Jody could tell Sabrina was learning fast, and all the girls wanted to help her.

One of the issues that Jody was covering was that there were reports of groundwater poisoning from Meth production somewhere in Chickasaw County. The runoff from the production of the drug is so toxic that it was poisoning groundwater springs that the local farmers were using to water their crops and feed their livestock. It was just a matter of time before the F.D.A. came in and told the farmers to destroy all their crops and that their livestock was not fit for human consumption. The local sheriff had been unable to locate the lab. Farmers were patrolling the area on four-wheelers, trying to find the source of the poisoning. Jody and the county cops were concerned that the farmers would take matters into their own hands and there would be deaths on both sides.

For the next hour and a half, the Mississippi Bobcats trained. The Bobcats ran and caught balls and enjoyed every aspect of being free to play and have fun. No child in the field exhibited more exhilaration than Sabrina. Sabrina seemed free for a while of the emotional incarceration of being the child caught in the middle of a nasty divorce. None of Sabrina's teammates knew precisely what caused her to feel and show her freedom on that day, but it did not matter as they all through her saw the need to reaffirm their feelings of freedom.

Chapter Eleven: The New York Interview

Viola sat behind her mammoth desk, staring at the rain clouds closing in on the New York skyline and fiddling with a gold pocket watch her father had once given her. The world only respects strength: remember, weakness and mercy are footnotes and anecdotal tails to be collected by historians and others who seek to collect trivia, which he had told her when he gave her the watch. The watch was the last passion of any monetary or sentimental value by a man her father had crushed and made destitute. Later, the former owner of the watch committed suicide, and Viola showed the article to her father.

Bryce Baxter sat in the quest chair facing her. At his foundation, Bryce was a handsome, preppy-looking guy, but today, he was diaphoretic and shaky. Bryce looked like he had slept in this good suit if he had slept at all.

"Look, Sis, you got to help me. The old man is livid."

"I am your half-sister. Stop calling me that, or I swear I will have you thrown out on your Ivy League ass." Viola spun around and shot an angry stare at Bryce. "Now stop your whining and tell me why you came here. I have a person to interview, and you are holding up on progress."

"Give me a job. You know, a mission, something I can tell the old man I help with so he can calm down. I got some faulty intel, and shit went sideways." Rattled and shaky, Bryce explained.

Viola turned back around to watch the clouds. She had always loved them. They were so capricious. No one told them what to design.

She had watched the clouds with Sabrina when Sabrina was a small child. Now, her daughter hated her.

"If you weren't his son, you would be at the bottom of the Hudson by now," Viola commented. "Why don't you talk to your real sister?"

There was a moment of silence between the two. "You did talk to Grace, and she won't help you. She wants you to drown in your own piss."

"Look. I know what you want most. You want your husband and little girl back. Tell me what to do, and I will help."

"You want to help. Get on a plane, go to some beach, and wait for my call. When I call, you had better show up and do whatever I ask, no questions. Now get the fuck out of my office. You are sweating all over my carpet."

MARCUS NEWPORT LED Shavon Crabtree into Viola's office. Shavon could not help but stare at Bruce's rumbled condition as he was leaving. Marcus handed Viola a file, and she began reading.

"I don't mean to interrupt, but was that poor guy applying for the same job?" Shavon asked in her country twang.

"No, that is my half-brother. He is in a twelve-step program, and he came here to make amends or some crap he did." Viola lied.

"Well, ma'am, I will say this is the most spectacular office I have ever seen. And I have never been flown to an interview in a private jet or driven in a limo. What exactly do you people do here?"

"We are a holding company. We hold financial interests in various companies and assure their profitability while increasing shareholder equity. Now, since this is my interview, may I ask a couple of questions?"

Marcus smiled, enjoying the contrast between the women, but said nothing.

"I see here your last employer was blown up in an organized crime-related car bombing; is that correct?"

"Well, I am fairly sure I didn't write it in an application that way."

"I also see the Missouri courts have an outstanding fine and cost of courts holding against you."

Shavon squirmed in her chair and looked to Marcus for help, but there was none.

"Well, ma'am, I have been a little short on funds lately, and I plan to clear that up as soon as possible. Life can be hard on a single girl in this world."

"I see the sheriff somewhere in Mississippi has a padlock on your trailer, and it will be auctioned off in about thirty days if you don't come up with fines plus interest."

"Well, this interview isn't going the way I hope it would." Shavon started to stand.

"Sit, we are not finished," Viola commanded.

Shavon retook her seat.

"If we hire you, I will pay your fines in Mississippi and Missouri. Also, I can have our legal team restate your license as a hardship case, and you will be operating before the end of the day."

"Ma'am, what job could make you so generous?" Shavon asked.

Viola knew her opening when she heard it and handed Shavon a picture of Vaughn and Sabrina. "These are my husband and daughter. I want you to keep an eye on them and report to Marcus." Viola pulled out another picture and handed it to Shavon. Shavon jumped when she saw the photo. "This is the woman who is working with Wade."

"Oh, Shit." Shavon dropped the photo of Jody Tyler like it was hot. "Ma'am, do you have any idea who this is?"

"Not a clue."

"This is Bull Tyler. I once saw her bulldog, a grown man."

"Bulldog?" Marcus had to know.

"This where you run someone down and grab them by the head and flip them over, using their own body weight to snap their neck."

"Good Lord, my daughter is in the hands of a Barbarian?"

"Did the guy live?" Marcus asked.

"He is in jail, paralyzed from the neck down if you call that living. But to be fair, he shot a cop and was escaping."

"Marcus put Ms. Crabtree on a plane back to Mississippi. Fix whatever you need to fix for her and give her some money to work with. Put some guys as backup in the area. I don't want her to get bulldogged while she is on the clock."

"I guess that means I got the job, huh?"

Chapter Twelve: When Women Collide

Jody knew Vaughn was aware she had been postponing a part of the investigation. Now, she could no longer delay. They had to visit Darius's home and speak with his wife. Jody had called the local sheriff to have deputies sent to the residence, hoping the show of force would cause Casandra to behave reasonably.

During the drive to take Sabrina and Vaughn home, Sabrina sat in the middle and fell asleep. Jody had been reared in a house full of children. She had sisters, brothers, nieces, and nephews, but something was building between her and Sabrina that she could not explain or understand. Jody had gone home alone and punched the heavy bag. She wanted to call her mother and hear her mom's voice, but thumbing through her ragged old bible was the closest she could do for the evening. Now, in front of her was a confrontation she hoped would never come.

The Youngblood home was a sizeable flat-frame home with a gate and porch on the front. Two deputies stood near their cars with their weapons drawn but not directly aimed at Casandra Youngblood, who stood in the doorway of her home with a double-barrel shotgun.

"I thought I instructed you guys to wait and observe." Jody scolded the older of the two deputies.

"We observed that she is sporting a double barrel shotgun, Detective."

Jody and Vaughn walked to the front of the gate and waited.

"If you don't have a warrant or some form of paper, I can shoot you for trespassing if you walk in my yard. The world would be out one whore."

Vaughn crossed over in front of Jody. "We haven't met. My name is Detective Vaughn."

"You aint a hard to look at, man. Are you sleeping with Miss Muscle Bound there? The only reason I ask is that we seem to have a history of sharing men folk, and maybe I should take you in and show you the ride of your life."

There was a chuckle from the two deputies but no response from Jody.

A small girl's tricycle caught Vaughn's eye, and Casandra noticed Vaughn's attention waiver.

"You got a little girl, don't you?" Casandra asked, reading something that flashed in the stranger's eyes.

"She is fourteen now. The time goes so fast. It won't be long before she takes on the world on her terms."

Vaughn opened the gate and stepped in. He reached down and touched the tricycle, and the rear wheels came off.

"She's been pitching a bitch for me to fix that. Damn, Darius aint been here, and the two boys we have follow him around like little puppies. When he aint here, they don't pay their little sister or me any attention at all."

"Here is the problem." Vaughn diagnosed.

"Well, I don't have the money to buy her a new bike."

"The bike is fine. This bolt is stripped. If you take it to a hardware store, tell them you need the exact same bolt. It should cost about fifty cents, and the bike will work like new."

"I guess all you men aint cut from the same cloth."

"Now, Mrs. Youngblood, someone told me you stood before God, your friends, and your family and promised to take Darius on as his wife."

"I did but you have no idea how bad he has treated me."

"I don't know that matters. The way I see it right now, he is missing, and what you have to do is let us talk to you. See, it is not about the bond between you and Darius but the bond between you and God. Now, I have two able-bodied officers here that are just standing around. They could be helping someone else solve some important, if not life-changing, problem. Yet here we all stand."

"Then I guess you had better come in and sit and ask your questions. You can bring your fallen woman with you." Casandra unloaded the shotgun and hung it over her arm.

Jody waved, and the deputies went back to their duties. Jody knew she and Casandra were approximately the same age, but Casandra looked and sounded so much older than she had when the two were girls in high school. The three children and the years of worry over a philandering husband had prematurely aged Casandra. Casandra won the battle by claiming Darius when Jody enlisted in the navy, but ultimately, she lost the war.

The Youngblood home looked like Casandra had given up on house cleaning. Food from half-eaten meals lay on the dinner table, and dishes piled in the sink. There was a broom that looked like it started to sweep the floor and then lost all volition. There were also piles of clothing in various stages of clean and unclean in piles around the house. Casandra moved a pile of laundry from a chair and motioned for Jody and Vaughn to sit.

Jody had never been prouder of anyone as she was right now with Vaughn. He had defused the situation.

"When was the last time you saw Darius?" Jody asked.

"Two days ago. I thought he was with you or some other whore out at his momma's old shack."

"Was he with Ricky?" Vaughn threw the question in to keep Jody from responding to the constant name-calling.

"You know Ricky?" Casandra seemed surprised. "Ricky was with Darius. Darius said he was working on a project that would get us on easy street, and Ricky was a big part of the plan."

"Did they say where they were going?" Vaughn asked.

"Said something about Tucker's bar up near West Point."

"New York," Vaughn exclaimed in total amazement.

Both Jody and Casandra laughed. "No, you sweet idiot, there is a West Point Mississippi in Clay County." Casandra corrected. "Do you think Ricky killed Darius and took off with the magic beans or whatever they were working on?"

"If we knew twice as much as we know now, we still would not know what happened," Vaughn answered.

"DO YOU THINK I AM A whore?" Jody asked Vaughn as they traveled toward West Point.

"You are not a whore."

"How do you know?"

"Because I am a former New York City Detective. No one in Mississippi knows whores better than me."

"Just checking." Jody was happy Wendy was picking up Sabrina to take her to practice with the Bobcats. It would be another long shift, and Jody wanted Vaughn to be there with her.

Chapter Thirteen: Tuckers Bar

"Well, it has been a long time since I saw you in here." Etta Mae Spain commented as Jody entered Tuckers Bar. Tucker's Bar was not precisely in West Point but on the outer rim. It was a working-class bar that catered to regulars. Etta Mae was a blues singer and part owner of the Bar. Etta Mae was in her mid-seventies but still had an attractive face. Etta Mae was slightly overweight but wore it well. The Bar began filling with people relieved to be off work.

"Where is that handsome father of yours? You know he used to come here to watch me sing the blues?"

"He is keeping pretty busy these days," Jody answered.

"You know, when he retired, we tried to get him to run for public office. But I don't think your momma would have any of that. Those golden years had been promised to her, and she was going to fight to savior every day she could."

"Momma is fine, too, since you forgot to ask." Jody turned and took Vaughn's arm. "This is Detective Vaughn; he is my partner."

Etta Mae walked over and stared directly into Vaughn's face. "You treat this one right. The Tylers are good people most of the time. This angel has had some tough times but has a loving heart."

Etta sat two cold beers in front of them without being asked.

"Do you remember seeing Darius in here a couple of nights ago?" Vaughn asked.

"Yeah. Darius was with Tasha Morehouse and that Ricky boy who follows him around nowadays."

"This looks like a busy place, even in the middle of the week. How do you remember?" Vaughn asked, picking up the beer and setting it back down.

"I remember because I had to ask him to step outside and conclude his business. Myron Rush and his crowd showed up, arguing about something related to money. I have a long-standing agreement with the locals. Even the gang banger wannabes, any business must be conducted outside, so we don't lose our license."

"How did that go down?" Jody asked, taking a sip of her beer.

"Smooth as silk. They walked outside and did not come back in all night."

"Have you seen Tasha in here since that night?" Vaughn asked.

"No, and she usually peeks her head through the door most nights just to check out the men folk. I don't mean to be catty, but that girl married young and now wants to get some of what she missed out on. If you get my drift."

A collective shiver ran down the spine of Jody and Vaughn. "Is her husband Joe still working the shop?"

"Yeah, he is there." Etta Mae answered.

JODY BEGAN TO THINK, for the days to be so long, this case was coming up fast. She drove to Joe's Auto Repair and parked her truck. There was no need to consult with Vaughn about what she was now thinking because the look on his face said he was thinking the same thing.

"I am so glad you are here, Bull. I mean Detective Tyler." Max, an older black mechanic, greeted Jody and Vaughn as they entered the auto repair shop. As many as a dozen cars of varied makes and models looked like they were in the process of being repaired, and another dozen outside looked like they were ready to be picked up. Jody had known Max from visits to the shop with her oldest brother, Norbert. Norbert owned the autobody shop in Lamont.

"Where is Joe?"

Max was covered in oil and grease. He showed signs that he had been doing the work of many, even with his advanced age. "He is upstairs. He got here before six a.m. Don't look like he slept a wink. He has been drinking all day."

"Do you know why?" Vaughn, mostly to confirm.

"That no account wife of his aint been home in two days. Man loves who and what he loves. There aint got to be no rhyme or reason to be had of it. He just does. He gives it all he has. Joe aint no Cassanova, but he is a provider. If it weren't for him, Tasha would have been turning tricks or slopping hogs, maybe a little of both."

Jody and Vaughn began walking toward the steps that led to the upstairs office.

"Bull, you being your father's daughter. It seems only fair to tell you he got a gun in there with him."

"But of course, this day is getting shittier and shittier by the minute," Jody whispered to Vaughn.

"Look at the bright side. We can skip the meetings later this evening if we get killed." Vaughn responded.

Joe Morehouse was a muscular man in the back, neck, and shoulder with a pouchier midsection. When Jody and Vaughn entered the office, the light was off, and a sad blues song was playing on a recorder. A narrow stream of the day's light silhouetted the room's occupants. Joe sat behind a desk that looked like it may have been the first thing he purchased forty years ago when he took over the shop from his father. Or maybe it was his father's old desk, but one of the drawers was open, and there was a 44. Magnum now showing. There was also a half-finished gallon of whisky on the desk and one glass.

"Hey Joe, long time no see," Jody called out.

Joe turned to look at Jody, but he was clearly drunk, and his eyes took time to focus. "Which one of the Tyler girls are you?"

"I'm Jody. When I was little, you let me change the oil in a car to win a bet with one of my brothers."

"I remember that your father was the chief of police." Joe slurred.

"Joe, my name is Detective Vaughn. We are here about your wife."

Joe snapped to focus on Vaughn but could not shake away the half gallon of whiskey. "How can a woman get out of her marital bed to pleasure a stranger? How can God make this even possible?"

"Joe, we are investigating a fire and need your help." Vaughn seemed to know instinctively it was his call to smooth the situation as much as possible. "Well, we need to eliminate some of the local women from the victim," Vaughn added.

"What are you asking me to do?" Joe asked.

"Give us a hairbrush or some item of clothing that we can use to scratch her off our list," Jody answered.

"Wait, are you saying my baby might not have left with another man? She might be the poor girl in an accident." Jody knew Vaughn had never used the word accident but was glad Joe had.

"We got to know," Jody answered.

Joe stumbled and retrieved a hair brush his wife kept in the office bathroom. Jody took the opportunity to remove the 44. Magnum from the desk drawer.

"If it is her, will you tell me?" Joe asked.

"We can do that, Joe," Vaughn affirmed.

Chapter Fourteen: A Shit Show and More at the End of the Line

Jody, not being a fan of fast food, was disappointed that it was the only option for her and Vaughn to make it back to the Lamont Police Department for their meeting. West Point, Mississippi, is about twenty miles from Lamont, and Jody and Vaughn made it just in time. Jody dropped Tasha's hairbrush off with the medical examiner to catch him before he left for the day. In the meantime, Vaughn and Singleton spoke privately.

When Jody got to the meeting room, it was filled with officers ready to proceed. She had overheard a rumor regarding Vaughn, and it was upsetting her. She wanted to ask him about it, but there was no time.

"Good, we are all here," Singleton stated agitatedly. "Detective Tyler, could you step this way, please?" Requested Lieutenant Singleton. Singleton stood in the doorway of an interview room at the Lamont Police Station. Beside Singleton stood Melrose Petty. Melrose Petty was a senior Detective from the Jackson, Mississippi, home office for the M.B.I. Jody and Detective Vaughn saw Petty just as they were ready to enter the conference room. Just as Jody and Vaughn approached Singleton and Petty, Casandra slithered out of the interview room. Casandra had tears in her eyes and tried to avoid eye contact with Jody and Detective Vaughn.

"This isn't getting any easier," Jody mumbled.

"Good police work seldom does, but every once in a while, we have the comfort of knowing we caught the bad guy—or, in some cases, the bad girl," Singleton stated.

Inside the interview room, a black woman in a business suit appeared to be completing some notes from the just-concluded interview.

"How tricks, Melrose?" Jody asked.

Melrose Petty was a large black detective with a built-in scowl. He had a solid sumo-like stomach and a muscular build, and he sat chewing on the end of an unlit cigar like a pacifier.

"Things are just fine. This is Octavia Drake, my new partner and one hell of a good detective."

Octavia smiled and nodded as she gestured for Jody and Vaughn to be seated. Octavia was a black woman with lighter coloring than the dark color of Melrose. Octavia's hair was braided and tied in the back. Octavia and slits for eyes that look more like they belonged on an Indian or Asian face.

"Detective Vaughn, you do not have to stay if you do not want to. We have a couple of questions for your partner." Singleton stated as she seated herself at the head of the conference table.

"No, I want him to stay. He is sharp and catching things that may be important to ending this mess as soon as possible. Besides, I think he has heard enough embarrassing things about me so far that if he were going to run away, he would have done it by now." Jody assessed.

"Detective, for the record, you are assigned to coordinate for the agencies interested in the explosion at Edgar Bend. Is that correct?" Octavia Drake dived right into questioning.

"Correct?" Jody one-worded it.

"Last fall, you took a course in explosive handling and disposal that the F.B.I. offered. Is that also, correct?" Octavia asked. Octavia's English was clear and crisp. No desirable accent or emotion could be noted in Octavia's voice when one was listening to her ask questions. Although

Octavia looked like any other woman in Mississippi, she sounded like she had been educated outside the Counties of Mississippi.

Jody took a moment to examine how Vaughn was looking at her. His look stayed the same. "Yes, that is also correct."

"Since taking the class was voluntary, may I ask what your motivation for taking the class was?" Octavia asked, and everyone in the room seemed to be waiting for Jody's answer and measuring how long it would take her to answer.

"Well, the instructor was cute, and I thought I might get to know him?" Jody answered right away.

"And did you?" Octavia asked.

"I don't know if that is our business since she answered candidly." Petty attempted to divert Jody's following statement.

"Now, Detective Petty, we are all adults here; there is no reason Detective Tyler should not want to answer," Singleton said with a smile.

"Well, the class was fun, and that all went well, but the guy had no interest in me for romantic proposes. As a matter of fact, he had no interest in any female for romantic purposes. And in my mind, I find that a real waste."

Jody could hear a muffled chuckle from Vaughn.

"When was the last time you had a romantic encounter with the deceased?" Octavia asked.

"When was Darius Youngblood declared dead?" Vaughn interceded.

"Perhaps I misspoke?" Octavia attempted to correct it.

"No, detective. You wanted her reaction to stating he was dead. That was a trick. Not a good trick, but a trick all the same. Not to worry, though. I am sure your trainer will advise you of better methods for subterfuge attempts when dealing with seasoned investigators." Vaughn defended, and Jody knew she had his support.

"It was about two years ago after I left the Navy," Jody stated.

"Why did you stop? Was it your idea or his to end the relationship? And I don't mean that to sound like a trick question." Octavia asked.

"My mother found out I was having an affair with a married man and asked me to stop."

"Are you in any way responsible for the two people murdered the night of that explosion and fire?"

"I am in no way responsible for the explosion that killed whoever was in that house."

Octavia turned and looked at Petty. "Have I missed any questions?"

"Just one. Are the Bobcats going to win against that Arkansas Corrections team this year?"

"Are you kidding? My girls are going to mop up the field with those ruffians." Jody answered.

"Well, I guess that means it is safe for Detective Tyler to continue her efforts to coordinate this mess." Singleton proclaimed.

"THANK YOU FOR HAVING my back in there." Jody and Vaughn were on their way to their desks.

"She is going to make a great detective someday, but she needs to learn a little bit more about deception," Vaughn stated.

"Melrose is a good trainer. He worked with my father years ago." When they reached their desk, Jody asked. "Do you think I am guilty of anything?"

"Yes, general shitty taste in men," Vaughn answered.

"I wonder if there is a support group or a 12-step program for that?"

NOW, IT WAS TIME FOR the tactical meeting. A large officer with a name tag that read Olsen stepped in front of a map and began. "We have located the meth lab. The problem is that it is mobile. That is why we have not been able to locate it. We know where it is now and must move on it tonight. The Governor is waiting for a confirmation that we have shut it down." Everyone in the room was glued to the presentation. "We are going to have officers breach from the front to block their access to the road. At the same time, officers will come down the back ridge, and we will trap them between the two units like rats. Any questions?"

"What do you think, Wade?" Singleton asked Vaughn.

Wade. Singleton using Detective Vaughn's first name seemed to electrify Jody, but she held it in.

"I don't like it," Vaughn stated.

"So, New York, show us country boys your stuff," Olsen stated and stood aside.

Vaughn sauntered up to the map and picked up a marker. "If they see us coming in the front, they will hit the woods and head up the ridge. We could spend all night wandering in the dark, trying to round them up. Also, if they had been there for a day, they could have set all types of booby traps in those woods. I don't know about country boys, but New York boys don't want to get caught in a bear trap."

The room started to laugh.

"So, what do you propose?" Olsen asked, now really listening.

Wade drew lines on the map and then numbered them. "We make noise like we are going in the front door. That is where they will expect us to come from. They most likely have an escape route that is not boobie trapped. We watch where they come out. We call out the number of the section where they are headed. Wrap up the escapees and lead troops down the same path they came out."

"And everyone goes home tonight with zero amputations. I like it." Olsen stated.

"DETECTIVE TYLER, I know you are upset with me, but I can't fix it if I have no idea what you are mad about," Vaughn stated.

Jody had not spoken a word to Vaughn after the meeting they stood on in the darkness, and she prepared for the false front door entry into the area of the meth lab. She pulled her hunting rifle from the gun rack.

"Upset. Wade. Do I seem upset, Wade? Gee Wade, you must be mistaken." Jody handed Vaughn the handheld radio.

"So, she called me by my first name, so what?"

"I have been stuck to you like glue for days, and I did not know you had a first name. When she said Wade, I thought maybe she was talking to a table lamp or a sock puppet."

Vaughn smiled. "I told you my first name the day we met."

"Okay, so I am a little jealous. And maybe I don't process emotions the best in the world. But I am still a person. Then I hear she asked you out."

"I turned her down."

"Don't do me no favors."

"I turned her down because of Sabrina and me. Sabrina is my priority right now."

JODY AND VAUGHN CRAWLED through the thicket of mud and leaves. Quietly, they approached the distant clearing. Jody made a motion for Vaughn to move close to her. There was something she wanted him to see. Vaughn moved up, and Jody pulled him even closer. They turned, and their faces were almost touching.

"I guess you have never been this close to your last partner," Jody whispered.

"No, but it's just as well. He was a 350-pound guy named Vito who always smelled like pastrami."

"Don't make me laugh. I am still not sure if I should be mad at you."

Jody and Vaughn crawled to a slight opening. "There where the tailers are, take a look. Take this." Jody reached into her pocket and retrieved a small item. There were three trailers converted into meth labs, and all were in total production.

"This is a night scope. Search the area over there while I search to the left." Jody began searching the night scope attached to the rifle she had carried from her pickup.

Vaughn had no idea what he was looking for, but he knew it when he found it. A person was guarding the path in front of them.

"I got one here and a second in a tree stand. I guess the idea was that if the cops had come through the front as Olsen had planned, the guards would have slowed them down long enough for the criminals to make it out the back." Jody's assessment tapered off as she saw someone she knew. "Myron Rush."

"The same guy that was talking with Darius and Ricky the other night," Vaughn whispered back.

"I am going to love talking with him." Jody aimed the hunting rifle. "Tell the guys to hold their position; I am going to make some noise."

Jody fired the rifle, and it sounded like a cannon in the night. Her shot was at a branch above the tree stand, and the branch collapsed and came down in front of the stand occupant. The occupant jumped from the tree and stared, running toward the trailers. Jody saw an old washtub sitting on the back of the trailer mount, and she shot the aluminum washtub. The tub banged and clanged and sounded like a marching band.

A group of men began running up a trail that could not be seen from the roadway. "Section Three. Close section three." Vaughn called out, and the escaping criminal ran directly into the waiting arms of the law.

OLSEN AND HIS MEN ROUNDED up fourteen of Myron's associates and handcuffed them, awaiting transportation. Myron sat handcuffed, leaning on the side of the trailer, trying to be invisible. It was no use as Jody walked up to him. "Gee, if it aint my old pal Myron."

"I aint your pal Tyler. Your brother had to stop you from killing me twice. Now I hear he left the state. I know you aint going to jack me up in front of all these witnesses."

Jody walked up to Myron and grabbed him by the ear. Myron screamed. "Myron, you got me all wrong. I am a changed woman. I have grown up a lot since I tried to drown you."

"Hey, man, this is some good cop bad cop shit; if you, her new partner, start doing some good cop shit." Myron cried out. Myron was a skinny kid who looked like the country rock band's poster boy. He had an oversized Adam's apple and a pock-marked face.

"What did we talk about last, Myron?" Jody asked.

Myron tried to look away, and Jody grabbed his right nipple through his shirt and started twisting it.

Many of the offices started watching with a look of humor on their faces.

"Make her stop, man," Myron yelled at Vaughn.

"Right now, she might be madder at me than you. I really appreciate you taking the pressure off me. So why don't you just answer her question."

Myron looked like he was about to cry. "I told you and your brother Lavon that I would not sell drugs in any of the 82 Mississippi counties."

"These nice police officers are carrying drugs and drugs, making shit out of your trailers, so don't tell me you are not making drugs."

"I did not say I was not making drugs. We don't sell drugs in Mississippi. We sell everything to those rednecks in Alabama."

Jody grabbed Myron by the face. "Listen to me, the stupid cocksucker, you are poisoning the groundwater in the Oktibbeha, and the Oktibbeha is mine. I won't let you kill babies on my watch."

"Did you kill Darius?" Vaughn asked.

"What? You trying to put a murder on me." Myron shrieked.

"The house fire this week at Edger Bend," Jody yelled. "People saw you arguing with him in Tuckers."

"I don't know who got toasted, but I would never kill Darius. He is working for me, and I saw him yesterday."

"What. You, lying piece of dirt, Darius is no dope dealer." Jody yelled. Jody began twisting Myron's nipple, so hard observers twitched and made faces.

"You right, Tyler, he aint. The work he was doing for me was legal. I been trying to buy the Betsey."

IT HAD TAKEN WHAT SEEMED like forever to process the fifteen criminals arrested at the raid. Even with everyone available to assist with bagging and tagging items confiscated at the raid, the night drew on, and Jody and Vaughn both were wired and alert into the early hours. Finally, a call came from a representative from the Governor's office, and they were thanked for their work and told to go home.

The Bobcats have a game scheduled for the following day, so when Jody was dropping Vaughn off at home, she decided to take Miss Addie up on her offer to stay in one of the boarding house rooms for the night. Jody had workout clothes in the storage compartment of her truck and was able to use the boarding house washer and dryer to wash her clothes. She was hoping to have the opportunity to apologize to Vaughn about her behavior earlier that evening.

Jody stood alone on the boarding house porch, wearing a sports bra and shorts, and staring at the night, wondering how she had made such a fool of herself. She wondered if her poor choices in men had tainted her view of all men. Wade was nothing like Darius, they were complete opposites.

For a moment, Jody thought she saw someone watching her on the road in the distance. Her interest in being watched was replaced with a warm feeling. The head-to-toe warmth you feel when someone special to you has approached from behind, and even though you have not turned around to greet them, their presence has already started to make you feel better.

"I don't know if I am sorrier that I mistreated you or made a fool of myself, and I have no claim on you whatsoever," Jody said, knowing Vaughn had approached from behind.

"Sometimes our jealousy gets tangled up in our concerns. The answer can't be to stop being concerned about others," Vaughn said, resting his palm on the small of Jody's back.

A shiver ran down Jody's spine, and she was compelled to turn around, grab Vaughn, and kiss him. First, she kissed him. Then he returned the kiss.

"Can you wait?" Vaughn asked as he pulled away slightly from Jody. You see, I got the little girl upstairs, and one day, she or her little girl is going to ask a question about how my marriage collapsed, and I want to tell them that I did everything right, step by step."

Jody could feel the sadness Vaughn was experiencing. "Do you remember the other day we were at the gas station, and that creepy cashier was saying those terrible things? You smiled? It was like there was another you trapped in the clever you. The other you deserve to live too." Jody turned with her back to Vaughn and wrapped his arms around her. "I have been in some tough spots before as a cop, but I was never as afraid as I was just then. I was afraid you would not kiss me back. I have heard guys say yeah, baby, my wife and I are getting a divorce, just trying to get laid. One thing I know about you is that you are not that guy. If you need me to wait or slow down, I will."

"I think you need to get some sleep. Your team has a game tomorrow."

"Yes, sir. But if you change your mind, I am in room nine." Reluctantly, Jody left the embrace and wandered back into the boarding house. Vaughn started to follow her, then stopped and looked into the night. There was someone out there, he thought, but who and why?

Chapter Fifteen: Sabrina's First Real Game

The Arkansas Timberwolves girls' softball team from the Arkansas Correctional Facility was quite different from the Bobcat team. The Timberwolves were like the image cast from a funhouse mirror compared to Jody and Wendys' team. The Timberwolves were currently incarcerated and arrived in an old sheriff's bus with bars on all the windows. The first person exiting the Timberwolf bus was a tall-looking guard carrying a shotgun.

The Bobcats played the Timberwolves twice the previous year and won both times. The Timberwolves worst enemy was themselves. The Timberwolves team argued and bickered among themselves and created nothing that could be vaguely mistaken for team spirit. During one game between the Bobcats and the Timberwolves, one of the Bobcat team members was at bat, and she hit a high pop-up toward center field. The girl working center field called the catch to stop the right and left fielders from running into her while she caught the ball. The Centerfielder missed the ball, and the Bobcat batter scored a home run. The left fielder then proceeded to punch and kick her centerfield teammate until the guard had to handcuff her and drag him off the field.

Attendance at Bobcat training was usually very weak. The number of people for this game was tremendous. Something about the potential for violence and random acts of volatility bought out people from far and near.

Aside from the Timberwolves' lexicographical attachment to vulgarity and their spontaneity of obscene gestures, the game went relatively smoothly. In the bottom of the ninety-inning, the Bobcats led 15 to 2.

Jody and Vaughn had been watching the game from the sidelines, and most of the action had been controlled by Wendy for the Bobcat team. In the top of the ninth inning, Bertha, the Bobcat right fielder, walked up to bat. It was clear the Timberwolves had been worn down. The Timberwolves pitcher threw a sweet pitch that seemed to hang over the home plate for a tenth of a second, and Bertha smacked the ball; it shot like a rocket through the left field gap past the shortstop and bounced wild. The shortstop spun on her heels and headed for the ball but ran into the Timberwolves Centerfielder. When the Timberwolves team members adjusted, Bertha was on the second plate and laughing. Bertha's laughter upset most of the Timberwolves and their coaches.

When Wendy approached them, Jody and Vaughn had been watching the game from the sideline. "I hope you two love surprises. I have a new stand-in batter," Wendy said with a grin.

Sabrina approached the batter's box and smiled at Jody and Vaughn. Jody looked too shocked to say a word and looked at Vaughn, who looked frozen in place. Sabrina cranked that bat as if preparing to launch the ball out of the park. The pitcher threw the first pitch and sailed directly over the plate. "Strike." The umpire yelled. Jody felt there was a scheme afoot. This was what made Wendy so good as a parole officer to her young clients. Wendy was part of a scheme that the Bobcat team could only have concocted.

The pitcher threw the next pitch, and Sabrina stepped forward and bunted the ball, and it bounced and rolled forward. The Catcher threw off the face mask and ran for the ball. Sabrina had already taken off and was running for first base. The Catcher located the ball and fired it toward first base. While running, Sabrina did not run to tag first and stay. Instead, she ran to round the first base and head to second, so the Timberwolf covering first base had to move over to tag Sabrina, but the Catcher threw the ball directly over the first base where no one was. The ball landed near right field. Bertha was on her way to home plate. Wendy screamed. "Stop on second, Sabrina." Not being able to hear Sabrina did not hear her, but the Timberwolves did. The girl recovering the ball fired the ball to home plate because she thought Sabrina would be stranded on second base. If she got the runner headed for home plate out, Betha, in any case, would be out at home plate. But the Catcher saw Sabrina rounding second and headed for third. The Catcher ran forward toward third plate to catch Sabrina in a squeeze play, but the ball was thrown behind her and shot into the dugout. The Catcher tried to correct the error by running back and diving headfirst into the dugout, but it was too late. By the time she got the ball and returned to home plate, Sabrina had slid into home.

Sabrina ran to her father and gave him a big hug. The Bobcats started celebrating their victory as the Timberwolves returned to their bus.

Jody once again had that feeling that someone was watching her. This time, she caught the culprit. She saw Shavon Crabtree staring at her from a distance as the spectators began leaving the grounds.

"Friend of yours?" Vaughn asked as he noticed Jody watching Shavon.

"She is bad news." Jody watched Shavon blend into the crowd of people leaving.

JODY AND VAUGHN LEFT Wendy with the Bobcats, celebrating their victory at a local pizza parlor. Sabrina stayed with her new friends while Jody and Vaughn went to the Lamont Police Station. They had planned to meet with a woman from the Department of Family Services who had been interviewing Dela. Mora, the Department of Family Services Worker, had requested a list of questions that Jody and Vaughn wanted answers to. Mora had requested that they meet at the police station as she was uncomfortable with the idea of meeting at the Futrell home.

"Let me start by saying Dela is very fond of you, Detective Vaughn." Mora started. Mora and Dela sat on one side of an interview table, and Jody and Vaughn sat on the other.

"My new partner has a way with women. A word to the wise." Jody joked.

Dela sat watching whoever spoke in her natural attempt to remain informed about what was happening.

"Dela has a formal eighth-grade education. She resents being referred to as a dummy. She wants to thank you for standing up for her."

"What did she see?" Jody asked.

"She has a condition before she allows me to give any information," Mora stated, and Dela nodded in agreement.

"What does she want?" Vaughn asked.

"Well, it would appear she has a secret hiding spot where she saves the proceeds from her labor, so to speak."

"And she doesn't want us to book her for solicitation. We have no interest in that." Jody stated.

"She also does not want you to discuss it with other cops because she fears they may steal her money, and she would have to start saving all over." Mora outlined.

"You are a very reasonable lady, Dela," Vaughn commented.

"Then we can proceed." Mora turned to Dela for confirmation. "The ground started shaking, and a bright light flashed. She also said a truck came down the cut-off right before the explosion."

Jody and Vaughn could hardly contain themselves, wishing they had heard the report firsthand.

"When she got to the area where the house exploded, there were two men who threw firebombs into the house. The tank exploded, and the blast knocked her down." Mora continued.

"The truck, what color was it, and did she see who was driving? Did they see her?" Jody tried to yank more information out of the Mora and Dela faster.

"The truck was black, and the driver was good-looking," Mora answered.

"It was Ricky's truck," Jody stated.

The remainder of the interview revealed a little more helpful information. When Jody and Vaughn left the meeting, a frail-looking man in a baseball cap stood in the middle of the police squad room. The man with the cap was staring at Jody, and he rushed up and handed her his card. "My name is Felix Wasserman. I work for the women's conference softball league." Felix took one step back and continued to eyeball Jody. "You are quite magnificent."

"Yes, sir, and you, may I say, are quite creepy," Jody said, taking a step back.

"I see what you mean about the little boy at the amusement park look," Vaughn said, half-joking.

"How can we help you, sir?" Jody finally asked.

"Well, I was with some associates today at the Bobcats and the Timberwolves game. We want to set up an exhibition game between your team and a conference team."

Jody and Vaughn both looked shocked. "Why?" It was the best Jody could come up with.

"It will allow the girls from the conference to learn by playing a team they know nothing about," Felix answered.

"Contact Wendy if she and the girls are a go for it; I am all in," Jody answered.

Jody and Vaughn had not planned to work that day, and the Bobcats game and pizza party took up much of their day. Still, the information that Dela had provided set them to thinking, and they briefly updated Singleton. Singleton had appeared on the news the night before in a short blurb about the busting of a major meth lab.

Chapter Sixteen: Shavon the Conspirator

"I am glad the client is happy with the pictures and how fast I got them," Shavon stated. Shavon sat across from Marcus in the restaurant of a roadside motel. Shavon was nervous because Marcus showed little or no emotion.

"The client is happy with your work and pleased that you were selected to assist on this assignment." Marcus took a drink from the tea that sat before him. "But don't you see how unhappy our client is that her husband appears to be fooling around, and the divorce is not yet final?"

"Well, Jody did not seem to me like she planned on sharing him with anyone, including his wife, judging from the photo of them kissing. And who knows what went on when they left the boarding house front porch."

"This Bull girl seems to come from humble beginnings. Do you think she can be persuaded to reason?" Marcus asked.

"Well, most of the Tylers are reasonable people right up to the point where they think the reason is not working."

"Stay by your phone. I may have an important task for you. In the meantime, I have forwarded those pictures you took of Vaughn and his mistress and the pictures of her daughter sliding in the mud to Mrs. Vaughn." Marcus produced the closest thing he could to a smile. "I must say I am personally pleased you asked so few questions about what is transpiring before you. May I ask why?"

"Well, Mr. Marcus, I think I learned in the last case that I worked it can be foolhardy to ask questions of the people who are paying a lot of good money for your assistance. You could end up getting shot in the ass or something."

Chapter Seventeen: Bribery at its best

Jody fired a left jab into the heavy bag being held by Tonetta. Tonetta was one of the firemen who worked with Bobby Joe. Bobby Joe allowed his sister access to the Firehouse gym. Tonetta went by the name Straight Razor; she was a paramedic firefighter who was good at her job but frequently exhibited issues with authority. Straight Razor was a thin, dark-skinned black girl with large eyes. She had a teardrop tattoo below her right eye and a heeled-over scar on her neck that made her look like the victim of a hanging.

Jody pivoted and shot two left jabs, followed by a resounding right hook to the bag.

"Stop dragging your left foot; you know what your brother said about that." Straight Razor reminded Jody. Jody's brother Lavon had boxed golden gloves and had worked with Jody and Straight Razor on boxing techniques. Now, Lavon was a detective in the small town of Shepherds Pass, Missouri.

"You are quite impressive." The compliment came from a man who had entered noticed. It was Marcus Newport, and he stood watching the women's train, waiting for a moment to interrupt. Marcus wore another of his elegant custom-made suits and expensive shoes. Straight Razor stopped holding the heavy bag and walked close to the intruder. She looked down at his shoes. "Maybe you should walk those sissy ass shoes back out of here before you get them all scuffed up."

"I was told I could find Detective Tyler when she is not working. I wanted to ask her a question privately about whether she would allow it."

"Hit the locker, Straight Razor. I will be just fine." Jody affirmed.

"You are even more stunning than photos reveal," Marcus stated as soon as Straight Razor was out of hearing range.

"Whatever you are selling, I don't want any."

"What about a Million Dollars."

Jody removed her boxing gloves and wiped her hands. Deliberately, she waited before responding. "What am I supposed to do for the million dollars?"

"Very little. Wade's wife wants him to take more time considering the divorce. The money to keep you from, shall we say, overly influencing his decision."

"I have heard of a lot of women being locked up for taking money for having sex. It sounds like you want to pay me a million dollars not to seal the deal with Detective Vaughn. That is rich."

"What has Wade told you about his wife? About his wife's family or about his life before miraculously showing up here."

Jody hoped the face did not give her away. She realized they only talked about her and the cases. Vaughn said next to nothing about himself. "Just because a man doesn't whine and bitch and moan about how bad a woman can treat a man doesn't mean he is hiding anything." The revelation came out of Jody faster than she meant it to. Was she charging into a conversation that was meant to deceive her?

"I worked with Wade a few times," Marcus revealed.

There was more shock in the comment than Jody could suppress. "You were a cop?" Jody questioned.

"No, Wade took a leave of absence from the police force a couple of years ago to help with some delicate matters in the company where his wife is Vice-President."

All the cards, Jody thought this bastard held all the cards, and what was worse was that he knew it.

"Two Million. Don't make a decision right now, just think about it. And in the meantime, use your detective instincts. Ask Wade a few questions about who and what he is."

"Keep your money. Not interested."

With that, Marcus was gone, but the dark cloud of doubt remained permeating the firehose gym.

JODY ARRIVED AT THE boarding house full of questions. She had spent the drive preparing for the worst. Jody wondered how she could make such bad choices regarding romance. Then, when Jody stepped from her truck, she saw Vaughn and Sabrina playing catch in the yard beside the boarding house. In an instant, none of what the stranger at the gym had told her made any difference. She knew that even if she had only known Vaughn for a few days, it did not matter. His true self was there playing with his daughter. And Sabrina was a barometer for who Vaughn had proven to be in the past. Yes, she thought he deserved to be heard out.

"Are you checking up on us on your day off?" Vaughn asked playfully.

"I was going to buy a dress for my brother's wedding, and I thought I would stop by. I got a visit from an old friend of yours this morning. He says you two worked together in the past."

Sabrina started signing to her father, and Jody had no idea what it meant.

"No, I am sure Detective Tyler would not be interested," Vaughn stated while signing the same to Sabrina.

"Okay, so what did I miss?" Jody asked, confused.

"Sabrina says that if you are going shopping for women's things, she would like to come along. I told her that would be an imposition. I would take her myself."

Jody smiled. "Look, Papa Bear, that is her way of telling you she needs a few things. She does not feel comfortable with you there watching her pick them out. You know, girl stuff. And I would love for her to come."

Sabrina ran to the boarding house room to get a few things and left Jody and Vaughn standing in the yard. Jody knew Vaughn could sense there were questions she wanted answered.

"This guy says you are not who or what you appear to be." Jody began.

"What do you think?"

"I think I wonder why your daughter is with you and not her mother."

For a moment, Vaughn searched his mind for the correct way to say what he had in mind. "Do you remember the night we went to the fire and the patrolman that called Dela, Dela the dummy, and she knew what he was saying?"

"Sure, but what does that have to with your daughter?"

"A couple of years ago, the company my father-in-law and his brothers own, which is the company my wife works for, had a problem, and they needed someone fast that they could trust."

"So, you took a leave and worked for the family business." Jody surmised.

"I did a good job, and my wife's father wants me to stay with the company and maybe help run it someday. He has a son that has been a total disappointment to him."

"Still doesn't explain why Sabrina is with you."

"The patrolman the other day had no idea that Dela understood him. My wife was putting in place a plan to destroy my career so I would come back to work for her father's company."

"Oh, my God, and your wife forgot Sabrina could understand what she was planning?"

"Sabrina is so pissed with her. I figured if they stayed separated until the device papers were finalized, it would give Sabrina a chance to calm down."

Jody could see Sabrina returning and knew she had to wrap it up. "So, how is it going so far?"

"I don't think she is mad at her mother anymore, but I think she has lost respect for her, and I only wish I knew the cure for that."

"She offered me two million dollars not to sleep with you."

Vaughn smiled. "You ladies have a good shopping trip."

JODY KNEW HER QUESTIONS about who and what Detective Wade Vaughn was had yet to be thoroughly answered. Something about a father helping his daughter learn the proper way to field a grounder had gone a long way toward disarming her mistrust.

Jody's shopping experience with Sabrina was fantastic. Jody had been correct in assuming Sabrina needed a few items she, as a teenage girl, did not feel comfortable explaining to her father. Sabrina had a credit card of her own that she used, and Jody was wondering if it was her place to ask if it was a courtesy card from her father or something her mother had given her.

Jody has six sisters and seldom has been the one allowed to lead the shopping expedition. This time, Jody was in charge, and she loved it. Many floor staff and salespersons referred to Sabrina as Jody's little sister, while others referred to Sabrina as Jody's daughter. Sabrina and Jody smiled at each other as though they were playing an elaborate prank on the familial constructs of those around them.

Jody was concerned that Sabrina and herself were building a relationship fueled by mutual admiration. Jody knew Sabrina needed a female in her life right now for emotional support, and Jody felt she was being thrust into this role.

One of the makeup associates talked Jody into sitting down so the associate could give Sabrina a lesson on how to apply makeup correctly. The makeup woman was a large-breasted woman reeking with cologne and had a German accent. Sabrina watched closely as the makeup girl added a simple makeup foundation before applying a blush. While Jody was seated, she started replaying her conversation with the man Marcus Newport. Out of the corner of her eye, Jody thought she saw Shavon Crabtree for a split second. By then, it was time for the mascara application, which caused Jody to lose sight of Shavon.

"Don't you think she looks stunning?" the makeup lady asked Sabina, and Sabrina nodded, having understood precisely what she was being asked.

"Now, her boyfriend will be unable to take his eyes off her." The makeup lady added.

Sabrina helped Jody select a dress for Lavon's wedding. Sabrina selected a matching dress, and they quickly became the stars of the sales floor. Jody was unsure if she could take Sabrina to the wedding in Shepherds Pass, but she knew she had to try.

DETECTIVE WADE VAUGHN stood transfixed, staring at the site of Jody when she was returning his daughter. Sabrina ran and wrapped her arm around her father like a younger child might, but who cared? She was proud of her makeup application on Jody.

"Mister, we still have some things to discuss, but God knows I like how you are looking at me right now."

Before Vaughn could formulate a thought, Jody's cell phone rang. "That was Shavon. She says she has some information on the case we are working on and wants us to meet her at Tucker's up near Clay County."

"Do I know Shavon?" Vaughn asked.

"No, of course not."

"Is she a friend of yours?"

"She punched my sister in the face, and the first chance I get, I am going to return the favor."

"Then, by all means, let's go."

Chapter Eighteen: Fire Fight at Tucker

As Jody drove to their meeting at the Tucker Bar, she and Vaughn discussed Marcus Newport. Vaughn told Jody that Singleton had called him and told him that due to their last report, she was having someone collect a sample to help the medical examiner determine if the body in the burned shack was Darius or Ricky Sells. Jody was distracted by Vaughn, occasionally seeking a glance at her.

"Did I really look that bad before?"

"Sorry. You were beautiful before, and you are even more beautiful now."

"And do you realize that it is technically still our day off? So why is she calling you on your personal phone?"

"I would like to think that it is for personal reasons, but the truth is she got interviewed by the news. I have seen people go crazy for their next shot at being interviewed."

"You think she has seen us as a way to bolster her career. And I should not be jealous?"

"Only if I should be jealous of that Felix guy."

WHEN JODY AND VAUGHN reached the Tucker Bar, Shavon was standing in front of the Bar. Shavon knobbed to acknowledge Jody; then she nodded to four men that were standing near a pickup truck.

Shavon then walked into the Bar. Jody started to get out of her pickup, and Vaughn grabbed her arm.

"Did you see that?"

Jody looked at Vaughn, wondering what she had missed. "What?"

"Is that the girl you came to meet?"

"Yes. Do you know her?"

"No, but she just tagged you," Vaughn noted.

"What are you talking about?"

"Street gangs do it in New York. Your friend knows who you are and what you look like. Those guys that were outside did not. She just marked you for them, so they know who you are."

It took seconds for the seriousness of what Vaughn was implying to sink in for Jody.

"Look, this place has a back door. I am going around to enter through the back. If I am just being paranoid, you can get a big laugh at my expense."

Jody looked at Vaughn, wondering what was going on in his mind, but she could not get the information she needed. "Okay, count to 20, then come in."

The moment Jody walked into the front of the Bar; an alarm went off in her head. This is all wrong, it shouted. Shavon was sitting with Marcus, staring at her from across the room. Marcus smiled, and a man with a sawed-off shotgun seemed to pop out of nowhere and pointed the gun directly at Jody. There was a loud boom, and the man's head seemed to explode as Vaughn appeared. Vaughn had shot the man with the sawed-off shotgun. A woman started screaming. The room was full of patrons trying to get out of the building as quickly as possible. People were being trampled, and Jody knew there were more shooters. Jody looked over and saw the woman who was screaming. The screaming woman was being held from behind like a human shield. Etta came out of the backroom carrying a case of beer and dropped the beer in excitement. The loud crash caused the man holding the screaming woman to look at the noise. The woman took the moment to run, and Jody fired three shots from her .45 in the center of the gunman that had been holding the customer. There as a refection in the mirror behind the bar it was a third shooter hiding behind the bar. When shooter three raised up to fire Jody and Vaughn opened fire and eradicated the man. Jody and Vaughn lost the fourth of the four men and Marcus in the mass of bodies rushing toward freedom. More importantly to Jody, Shavon was also nowhere to be found.

THE STATE PATROL HAD begun to arrive to help contain the Bar, which was now a major crime scene.

"What are you looking for change for a five?" Jody asked Vaughn as she saw him going through the pockets of the now almost headless gunman.

"Where is the Sunview Motel?" Vaughn asked.

"A few miles down the road, why?" Jody asked.

"This guy has a room key."

"Damn. One thing for sure about your partner: no matter what anyone says, you are a cop. I am going to get someone over there to watch the place and, if our party shows up, to follow and not engage."

Etta Mae surveyed the mess that was her Bar, then walked behind the Bar and grabbed a bottle of whiskey. "Do you, too, want to join me?" Etta Mae seemed not to be phased by the chaotic scene.

"I am sorry we had a gunfight in your bar, Etta Mae," Jody stated.

"Sorry. Why? This is like old times," Etta Mae responded, then looked at Vaughn. You know the Tylers are decent and respectful folks most of the time, but not always."

Vaughn stopped scribbling in his notepad. He knew a story was coming, and he wanted to hear it. Vaughn also knew that even though Etta Mae was pretending no to be mad she was. Her release would be like that of an angry aunt. Controlled and focused not to severer a lifetime relationship but still focused enough to get her point across.

"You know all the Tyler boys are a lot like their father. Some by nature, and others had to work at it a bit. But our dear, sweet Jody is like her father and never had to work at it a day in her life." Etta Mae knocked back a shot of the whiskey. "So, has Jody had the chance to tell you what her brothers did to Darius?"

"Please stop, Etta Mae. If I could have avoided this circus, I would have. And that tale is not all true."

Etta Mae knocked back another shoot while watching emergency crews work on injured patrons. "You see, back when Darius was younger, he was quite the scamp. He managed to score on your partner in a biblical way if you get my drift."

Jody looked away, trying not to look at Vaughn. They were making progress now. More of her dirty laundry was starting to show.

"Her brother found out."

"Which brother so far I haven't stood a chance of keeping up?" Vaughn asked.

"That maniac Norbert. Norbert rounded up the brothers, and they kidnapped Darius and stripped him and tried him to a railroad track."

"Please tell me this is a Southern joke." Vaughn looked between the two women and knew it was true.

"So, what happens?" Vaughn asked.

"Darius was blindfolded. He was tied to the track next to the one the train ran down, so he heard the sound of the train and the vibrating. Later, they made him walk home in his underwear." Jody explained.

"And at least one of these guys is a cop," Vaughn confirmed.

"Coffee break is over. Your boss wants your assess at the Sunview motes asap." An angry-looking patrolman announced to Jody and Vaughn.

THE SCENE AT THE SUNVIEW Motel was, if not more remarkable, equally horrific as the one that Jody and Vaughn had just left. A deputy lay face down in a smear of his own blood while a circle of cops in varied uniforms stood in a circle over him. A second deputy was being wheeled off on a gurney by paramedics.

"Hotshot, State Detectives, what do you clowns do for your next act?" One of the cops circling the deceased called out.

"What the fuck did you say?" Vaughn yelled.

Jody tried to grab Vaughn's arm, but he pulled away.

"I said you guys need to get a handle on whatever the fuck you are working on or call in someone that knows what the fuck they are doing." A red-faced Cop screamed back at Vaughn.

"Do try to push the blame off on someone else because you screwed up. I was standing beside my partner when she specifically instructed officers to find and follow. That is because she knows that if a group shoots its way out of one exchange, they are likely willing to shoot their way out of another."

"We aint a bunch of water boys."

"And it is a good thing from what I have seen so far, you are not fit to carry Detective Tyler's water. Balls and superior force can get you a winner. One without the other makes you guys a bunch of fucking pallbearers."

"I could not have stated it better myself," Singleton stated from inside the motel. "Detectives, if you would please follow me."

Sington turned around and walked back into the motel. There was a man from the medical examiner's office kneeling over the body of an old man who was covered in blood and had expired. "Ugly, but not why I call you inside." Singleton turned and walked to one of the rooms. The room was filled with police and emergency staff. There was a young woman lying naked, face up on the floor. A shotgun blast had almost totally removed her face.

"Is this, by chance, your friend Shavon?" Vaughn asked.

"Shavon is not my friend. She was engaged to my brother."

"Norbert?" Vaughn asked.

"No."

"Lavon?" Singleton asked.

"No."

"Bobby Joe?" It was Vaughn's turn to guess.

"No Lovester," Jody answered.

"This family tree shit is giving me a migraine. Just tell me why she lured you into a gunfight." Singleton complained.

"I am more confused about why she is hanging out with an associate of Detective Vaughn's soon-to-be ex-wife," Jody stated.

"Come again?" Singleton asked.

"When we entered the bar, the guy that offered me two million dollars to get Detective Vaughn to go home to New York was sitting there."

"Maybe you should have taken the money. You turn down something like that; the party offering knows there is only one way to deal with you." Singleton surmised.

"Role her over." Jody instructed the medical technician, preparing to put the young woman in a rubber bag."

"Why." The technician asked.

"Because I want to get a good look at her ass," Jody answered.

Singleton stared at Vaughn as if he had the answer to a question she had not asked.

The technician complied.

"It's not Shavon."

"Are you sure?" Singleton asked.

"Yeah. Shavon has three holes in her ass."

Now, the technician, Vaughn, and Singleton were staring at Jody.

"Shavon got shot in both cheeks by twenty-twos. The third hole is the one mother nature put there."

Chapter Nineteen: Say it in the Night

"This almost reminds me of the end of a naughty teenage date," Jody said to Vaughn. The two sat in her truck outside the boarding house where Vaughn was staying. They had said little during their drive. Each revelation into the cases they were working on brought them closer to knowing each other, and the path was frightening in some ways.

"Well, considering we just left two crime scenes riddled with dead bodies, got our ass chewed off by the local cops, and are no closer to figuring out if Darius is still alive pretending to be Ricky or if Ricky decided it was time to stop taking sloppy seconds and worshiping at the feet of the master, you must have been a hell of a teenage date."

"Right back at you." Jody smiled. "For some reason, I feel like I am lying to you when I don't tell you things that may have nothing to do with the case."

"Such as."

"The story about my brothers tying Darius to the railroad track. There was a little more to it than that."

Vaughn turned and faced Jody, taking her hands to give her strength to complete whatever she was going to tell him.

"Darius had bragged to his friends that on that night before the daylight, he would deflower not one but two Tyler girls and therefore create a place for himself in the unwritten Lamont Mississippi record books."

"I think I am starting to understand why you did not want to discuss this. It shines a light on more than just yourself."

"Well, the other Tyler girl was Anita. I am three years older than her, meaning she was fifteen at that time."

"Oh, shit, you did it to prevent him from doing her first in an attempt to get him to change his mind."

"Exactly. That and to defy Norbert. Norbert was overprotective back then."

Vaughn sank into the seat, staring into the night, where the envelope of day threatened to pierce its way through.

"So now you know all my dirt, tell me about your wife." Jody sat back in the driver's chair, bracing herself for the worst.

"I think my wife has lost her mind." Vaughn paused and then continued. She has always been a tough, self-reliant businesswoman, but a couple of years ago, she and her father started making up the rules as they went along."

"What did you do for them when you worked for them? You and the Marcus?"

"I arranged meetings for groups that were less than friendly to one another."

"You mean like setting up gang intervention meetings on a corporate or global level?"

"Exactly."

"So why did you let me think you were an international assassin or worse?"

"Because you compel me, and I don't know how to handle it. I am not the most exciting guy in the world. Bad boys seem to be more your speed."

Jody hugged Vaughn. "You guys can be such idiots."

"Thank you, I think."

"When you were talking to Casandra about death, do you part that was just as much about you as about her? You gave your wife every chance you could."

"I love who she was. She is no longer that person. I hate the person she is now because I feel like that person consumed the one, I loved." Vaughn whispered into the night.

Chapter Twenty: The Plight of Dela

"What did she do wrong?" Bryce asked. Bryce sat across from Viola Vaughn in one of the company jets. Bryce had been retrieved from the Miami Hotel, where Viola had sent him to rest. Bryce looked anything but rested. There were rings under his eyes, and he stank.

"You don't get to ask that. You came to me to get my help with the old man. If you are too chickenshit to do this job, let me know. I will inform our dear father that, once again, you have failed to be a real man." Viola poured herself a drink and took a long swallow.

"I am just saying this is not the type of thing I usually do."

"No. I remember that young boy prostitute in Mumbi you kill for laughing at you. And the peasant in Inda who wouldn't stop screaming at your fucked up driving until you bashed in his head. Maybe you should pretend you are in one of your drunken drug induced rages and score some points with the old man all in one fell swoop."

"I am just saying if Wade doesn't want shit to do with you anymore, is killing this woman going to change that?"

Viola lunged forward and grabbed her half-brother by the shirt, grabbing his shirt, hair, and skin. She stared directly into Bryce's eyes, and the intensity of her stare made the color of her eyes seem to change. "Listen to me, you pathetic cocksucker. I don't have to explain to you or anyone else what the man means to me. I want my husband back. Now that may not be possible but if I feel that you or anyone else got in the way of my best efforts to reconcile, my father will be the least of your worries. And as far as killing this tramp I don't care if I have to order the execution of everyone in that disastrous little state to make that work."

Now all Bryce wanted was to get out of the craft. A deal any deal it did not matter, Viola was in full rage.

THE CONVERSATION THE night before had gone a long way toward improving the working relationship between Jody and Vaughn. They had realized the medical examiner was not only stuck as to identifying the male remains from the fire, but the examiner was now flooded with new bodies to examine. Jody and Vaughn revised Casandra and Ricky's girlfriend to collect hair samples. They were hesitant to do this in the first interview because it may have caused undue panic, but it was now evident that the problem was increasing.

"Alright, we want everyone to get up and walk outside and stand clear of the building." An officer in bomb disposal armor walked up to where Jody and Vaughn were seated, reviewing information.

"Is this a practical joke?" Vaughn asked.

"Our bomb techs don't have a sense of humor."

"Lovely."

THE BOMB TECH SEARCHED the building while all the members of the Lamont Police Department stood outside. Prisoners and those being questioned were held under guard on armed transport buses while the process took place. News crews started to surround the mass of confusion being generated. Finally, Sargent Massey, the bomb tech leader, carried a package and handed it to Jody.

"What the hell is that" Jody asked. It was a small package addressed to her with no return address.

"We had metal detectors and x-ray machines set up in mail receiving. Whatever this is made the machines go crazy." Massy answered. "If you girls are ordering sex toys and you don't want your husbands or boyfriends to know, please have them sent somewhere else." Everyone started staring at Jody. Jody turned around, and for the first time, she saw a genuine laugh coming from Vaughn. Jody ripped the package open and inside was a rusted horseshoe.

"Can we go back inside now? I was waiting for a call back from a lead on a murder case we were working on," Vaughn asked.

Jody stood for a moment, thinking about what the horseshoe meant. Jody now had a piece of the puzzle.

BORIS SAT IN THE CAB of his rig, zipping up his pants. Dela sat beside Boris, wiping her mouth. "Oh, God, you are so good at that. I wish you could teach my wife, and I would never have to stop by here. What I really wish you could teach my wife is not to talk. That would really be worth the money." Dela started to exit the truck, but Boris stopped her and handed her additional money. "This is because you never try to squeeze money out of people. I appreciate you." Boris was a huge man with a Russian accent. He is one of Dela's regulars. Dela's made it a point to watch out for Dela and the other truck stop girls.

"Hey, pretty lady, would you like to make some cash." Dela saw a man in a shiny suit waving a wad of hundred-dollar bills. She thought the money would be nice. The man was no one Dela had ever seen before. He was sweating profusely. The man was standing by the ladies' room for the weight station. Dela came closer, and the man reached out to grab her. Dela struggled to get free. Whatever he had in mind, she wanted no part of it. The man slammed Dela into the brick wall and shoved her into the lady's room. The man was Bryce. Bryce pulled out a Randell Combat knife and drew back the blade to shove it in Dela, but before he could complete his downward thrust, Boris grabbed his hand. Boris had been watching Dela walk away and saw her shoved into the lady's room. Boris squeezed Bryce's hand, and the knife fell to the ground. Boris grabbed Bryce by the throat and slammed him against the wall. Dela struggled to her feet and wrapped herself around Boris from behind. "Don't worry Dela, Mississippi got places for creeps like this."

JODY SAT THINKING WHEN to tell Vaughn what the horseshoe meant. Vaughn had finally received the calls he had been waiting for all morning: one from the Gaming Commission and one from the Department of Transportation.

A clerk walked over to Jody and Vaughn and stated. "The cops out near the weight station just arrested a guy, and he won't say anything to them. He says he only wants to talk to you, and he says he is related."

"Gee, which one of my knucklehead relatives got arrested now," Jody asked.

"Not you this time, sweetness; it's your partner's relatives."

Vaughn was stunned.

"This I got to see." Jody cheered.

BRYCE WAS BEING HELD in the Leflore County, Mississippi jail, a monolithic white stone structure with more than its fair share of bars. This building was built long before central air conditioning even hit the drawing board. The sergeant of the floor walled Jody and Vaughn to the holding cell, where Bryce sat on a metal structure masquerading as a bed. A lidless aluminum commode was in plain view, and the cell was unobstructed from all the other cells in the room.

"Wade, get me out of here." That was the first thing Bryce said.

"Your buddy tried to knife a working girl that goes by the name of Dela. He was carrying over ten grand in a gold money clip and had a watch that cost more than my car. I have not taken the detective examination, but I think something fishy is going on here." The sergeant outlined.

"You must be the farmer's daughter causing this mess." Bryce accused Jody.

"Me. Sir, we have never met." Jody responded.

"Are you too freaking dim to know how to play the game? Marcus offers you two million. You say no, I want twenty. He then says five. You say fifteen. He says ten, and then you say done. He hands you a bag with ten million dollars in it, and everyone is happy."

"That's stupid."

"Lady, what is stupid is you can't tell the Marcus of the world no deal I won't negotiate. They only exist because of people who refuse to negotiate."

There was the sound of a man screaming in pain somewhere unseen.

"And what the hell is that?" Bryce asked.

"The rack." The sergeant answered and smiled. "Just joking. They won't let us use the rack much anymore."

"And don't call me lady. My name is Detective Tyler."

"If you value your nipples, you would do well to remember that" Vaughn informed Bryce.

"This place smells like men's balls. Get me the fuck out of here." Bryce screamed.

There was another blood-curdling scream in the distance.

"How is my wife?" Vaughn asked.

"Don't be ridiculous that bitch has lost her mind. And our father is in China somewhere. The only one that stands a chance of controlling her is you."

"What do you want us to do with him?" The sergeant asked.

"You got him, you; you got the knife and a witness. Process him." Vaughn answered, then turned to Bryce. "See you in ten to twenty."

"I think it's time we visit the Betsey."

THE RIDE TOWARD BETSEY seemed long, and Jody could tell that Vaughn was expecting all the road work and construction along the way. She wanted to discuss it with him but was still wondering how much she should tell him about the horseshoe. The silence of the drive had taken its toll, and Jody had to speak. "When are you going to explain to me why your wife now wants to kill Dela?"

"Maybe I should wait until you tell me why Darius sent you a horseshoe."

"Did anyone ever tell you that you are too smart to be a cop?"

"Sometimes, when people like each other a lot and don't know each other, they do not always know what is important to tell the other. I am not hiding anything valuable from you. If you feel the need to hide things from me, it's alright. It does not change the way I feel about you. I trust you."

Vaughn's comment felt good, but it also stung a little bit. Jody wondered if she was having trouble letting go of her past mistakes and keeping the lessons she had learned from them.

"He wants me to meet him alone. So, he can explain."

"Jody, if you go alone, you will die."

"WELL, I WILL BE DAMN. I know who you are. You are one of Sam Tyler's girls. It has been a coons age since I saw you last. My how you have filled out. Does and old man's eyes well." Rex, the owner of the Betsey, stated as he plopped down in his chair. Jody and Vaughn had been led to the back room of the Betsey by a woman who was cleaning everything that looked like it may have ever been touched by human hands. The woman wore large green cleaning gloves and sprayed and wiped even as she guided the detectives to Rex's office. The Betsy was different from the Tucker Bar. The Betsey was a bar that had serviced truckers and had a huge parking lot that was filled with potholes. The Betsy was surrounded by a field that was at rest from farming.

"How is the little sister of yours, Anita. Is she still in the army?" Rex continued.

"Yes, the last time I heard, she was overseas and due to return to be released," Jody answered.

Rex looked at Vaughn with the assurance Vaughn would appreciate his next comment. "That Anita is some piece of work. She would clean guys out in the back poker room while talking football."

"I am looking forward to meeting her someday," Vaughn assured.

"I guess you guys came to ask me about Ricky Sells. You know, I had no idea he worked at a gas station." Rex commented.

"Hold on, how did you know we had questions about Ricky Sells?" Jody asked with a look of confusion that mirrored the one on Vaughn's face.

"It was just on the news. They identified his body as the body that burned in the house fire. That chubby little policewoman that is running the case was interviewed on the news." Rex revealed.

"And you wonder why I don't like her," Jody whispered to Vaughn.

"We had questions about Darius Youngblood," Vaughn stated.

"Yeah, not there is a man's man if ever there was one. Surprising, too, because I remember when his mother used to bring him around here. He was always getting into trouble."

"Slow down. I am new in town. Why would Darius's mother bring a child to a bar?" Vaughn was flabbergasted.

"She did accounting for many of the small businesses in the area. Darius followed in her footsteps. He may seem dumb, but he knows his way around numbers," Rex stated.

"Damn, I guess I didn't think that mattered." Jody realized.

"Course, it matters. That is how he was able to put a bid on this place. My wife and I are retiring in Florida."

Vaughn chucked. "Can I see the papers?"

Rex was an overweight man with a heavy grey beard. He wore a plaid shirt that made him look like a lumberjack in a TV ad. It took Rex a while to recover the paperwork and hand it to Vaughn.

"Did you ever notice Darius in here with Tasha, the girl from the fire?" Jody asked.

"Every time I saw Tasha in here, she was with Ricky. When they were with Darius, the other girl was with Darius."

"What other girl." Jody and Vaughn stated in unison.

"You know her, the one whose family lost their land near Edger Pass. Come to think of it, they still call the pass by the family name. Now, what was it?" Rex said, trying to scratch the answer out of his memory.

"Crabtree," Vaughn stated.

"Hold on, are you telling me Shavon has been screwing Darius?" Jody called out.

"Now who leaves their underpants where is none of my business. By the way, good luck with that ballgame against that conference team."

"What?" Jody exclaimed.

"Yeah, that cop leading the investigation mentioned that your Bobcats is going to pay a conference team, and they expect the governor to be there."

"I hate her," Jody muttered.

"Which one Shavon or Singleton?" Vaughn asked.

"Pick one."

"LOOK, JODY, YOU HAVE got to see the irony in this whole mess. My wife is an Ivy League graduate and a prominent businesswoman.

She has her personal private investigator find someone local to shadow us and ruin our case, so I go back to her. The person her investigator hires is banging the person of interest we have been trying to locate."

Jody and Vaughn sat in the traffic jam on their return from Betsy. "Could you please use a different expression other than banging? I know you are from New York. Never mind."

"Feelings are not something we turn on and off. I was not trying to make fun of you. Please don't go see Darius alone; it's a trap."

Jody quietly continued the drive, praying that her passion toward Darus would evaporate, or at the least not drive her to make another wrong choice. In her mind, she was becoming aware that she thought Darius was a victim. Maybe he had played fast and loose with Myron and his thugs, but now he was in too deep, and it was her responsibility to ride in and rescue him. But was she now engaging in the same bone-headed thinking Tyler girls had always accused the Tyler men folk of engaging in?

Vaughn saw the funk Jody had descended into and reached over and touched his hand. "Look at the Brightside. At least we are probably having a better day than my brother-in-law, Bryce."

Chapter Twenty-One: How to Arrest a Ghost

"We are not going to try to arrest a ghost." Vaughn signed and told Sabina. Sabrina had been trying to follow the conversation between Jody and Vaughn by lip reading, but there needed to be more in her understanding.

"Alright, sit, and I want your father to sign what I tell him." Sabrina sat. Vaughn and Jody had returned to Vaughn's room at the boarding house and were preparing to find Darius.

"In the United States, there are ghost towns. These are towns that are abandoned for one reason or another. Some because they were there for temporary purposes, others because the chief industry died out." Jody checked to be sure Sabrina and Vaughn were following her. "In Mississippi alone, there are over fifty ghost towns. Many were abandoned because they were no longer viable after slavery, after the Civil War ended, or after the railroad was run. These abandoned towns still are the property of someone, so people are not allowed to go there without permission."

Sabrina began signing something.

"She asked why the two of us?"

"Because the ghost town that we are going to is in what is called an unincorporated area, as many such towns are. That means no police, no sheriff, or government of their own. That puts them in the jurisdiction of the State Police. We are state Detectives."

Sabrina began shaking he head, and Vaughn signed Jody's answer.

"I don't think that is what she is asking." Vaughn assisted.

"The guy we need to see is an old boyfriend of mine, and we used to sneak in where we were going to meet," Jody answered, hoping her answer would help Sabrina understand while not hurting the feeling Vaughn was developing toward her. "Sabrina, I promise I will do everything possible to keep your daddy safe." Sabrina hugged Jody, and there was a transfer of energy from person to person. Jody wondered how a mother could ever deny herself this contact.

THE SMELL OF MOLD AND rotted wood competed with the official town smell of San Locos. San Locos was the remains of a time long past. It once had been the depot for the Union Army to store supplies during the Civil War before long campaigns. The buildings all faced a center street and were in various stages of decay. The town looked like the ghost of an old marshal might walk out at any minute and challenge an outlaw to a gunfight. At one end of the street was a rickety building, a sign that read Horseshoe Saloon, and a dim light came from within.

"Is it just me, or is this creepy?" Vaughn asked as he drew his service weapon.

"It was exciting and sexy when you were a starry-eyed teen," Jody answered.

"You must have caused your mom hell."

"Mom was a schoolteacher."

"I thought so. The way you explained the ghost town thing to Sabrina was excellent."

"Nice to finally meet you. You must be quite a guy. Your wife is willing to pay millions to have you back and is hell-bent on destroying this great state if it stands in her way." Darius sat in the shadows of a flicker oil lamp. Darius poured himself a drink. He stood behind the old bar like a bartender.

"Darius Youngblood, I am here to escort you to the Lamont Police station for questioning regarding a double homicide. If you wish, you can arrange for legal counsel to be present before questioning," Jody stated in a cold, modulated tone.

"I should have known you would not have come alone. Is he, my replacement?"

"There is no need to be rude, Darius," Jody responded.

"She is quite the woman, don't you agree, Detective?"

Jody was now wondering if Darius was angering Vaughn.

"You know we are a lot alike." Darius took another drink.

"Not at all. You are sloppy, and you made mistakes." Vaughn stated.

Jody was confused about what Vaughn was seeing that she missed.

"Do tell. So, outline what I did wrong for me."

"Well, first, you probably planned to rip Myron and his idiot thug bunch for every dollar that had. Then you planned to turn over the location of their meth lab to the cops or turn them over to the farmers and have them executed." Vaughn began.

"Well, they were poising our water, aint that right, honey bunch."

"Then, when you began reviewing the paperwork and found out that Rex liked the idea of retiring and some of the surrounding farmers were willing to sell off their portions of their land, you realize the deal could really work."

"What?" Jody was shocked.

"You see, Detective Tyler, the road construction we were stuck in is where they are building a highway innerbelt that will take millions of people past the Betsey. I checked. I also checked the gaming commission. You have been making inquiries."

"Man, this guy is almost as smart as your brother Lavon." Darius praised.

"All this was about building a resort like Vegas?" Jody asked.

"No, more like Reno and I would own the whole thing."

"I see why people can't wait to tie you to a train track," Vaughn commented, and it angered Darius. Darius walked from behind the bar.

"Since we are sharing the truth, what did you hear about that maniac tying me to a train track?"

"That you got tired to an abandoned track and made to think you were on the live track," Vaughn answered. "I guess that made you piss yourself or worse."

"Bull shit," Darius screamed. "That is what the Tyler boys told their sisters. The truth is they tied me to the live track and snatched off the hood so I could see the train coming. One of her brothers chickened out at the last minute and sent the train down the other track."

Vaughn started laughing. "They should have let you die. Then Ricky and Tasha would still be alive."

"That Anita Tyler would have been such a treat." Darius sneered.

Vaughn punched Darius in the gut and fell to one knee. "I may not be the account you are, but if my math is right, if Jody was turning 18 and Anita was three years younger, that means she was 14 going on 15 years old."

Darius coughed and wheezed. "Gee babe, he hits almost as hard as you do."

"That one is from all the fathers with daughters that are 14 and 15."

"You killed them?" Jody asked.

"He wanted time work is the plan. He had been grooming Ricky for the kill all along."

Darius struggled to his feet, reached over, and opened one of the shutters leading to the outside. There was a rifle shot, and it shattered the mirror behind the bar, and the reflection, Jody, sank onto the floor as the real Jody and Vaughn dived for cover.

"Handcuff him," Vaughn commanded, and Jody was already handcuffing Darius to the metal post beneath the footrest at the bar.

Jody crawled to the doorway, were Vaughn crotched. "Well, Mr. Mental Heavy Lifting, what do you think?"

"Well, you might not like it, but here goes. There is more than one. They are using rifles; our handguns are no match. They want us to empty our bullets into the night air."

"Makes sense, so what is the solution."

"Give up," Darius answered.

"Well, I still have this." Vaughn reached into his pocket and pulled out the small night scope Jody had given him. I will find a lane to run in that is out of their line of fire. While they are shooting at me and trying to adjust their vantage point, you are going to run to your truck. The handheld radio we were using is on the truck's floor on the passenger side, away from the gunfire."

Jody knew he had expertise when it came to being under fire. She kissed Vaughn and hugged him. "Remember, we still have a deal to seal when those divorce papers are signed, so don't get anything shot off you might need."

The first part of the plan went exactly as Vaughn had predicted. When he located a lane where he could not easily be shot, he ran to it. The shooters seem to ignore the fact that his run has no goal or advantageous destination. Jody slipped out and ran for her truck. One of the shooters saw her just as she was reaching the vehicle. The shooter opened fire and shot out the driver's rearview mirror. Jody commando crawled to the passenger side and opened the door. This turned the overhead light on, and the shooter shot out her front windshield. Jody spotted the radio, now covered in glass shards. She looked, and the rifle she had used the other day was still in the gun rack, with the night scope attached. Jody took a deep breath and retrieved the gun. She then crawled back to the rear of the truck. Jody lined up her shot perfectly, squeezed the trigger, and took out one of the shooters.

Multicolored lights began to flash, and a siren started to blare. Someone had reported the gunfire, and the State Patrol was responding. The patrol car came to a drastic stop, and two officers jumped out with their guns aimed at Jody. "M.B.I." Jody yelled, raising her badge from her belt. One of the officers was short and thin. Jody threw him her rifle. "If anyone tries to shoot you, shoot them back." The other officer was tall and lanky. "I got prisoner in there handcuffed to the floor rail. See if you can make him comfortable. Jody drew her .45.

"Where are you going?" Lanky asked.

"There is at least one more shooter, and my partner is out there in the field."

"Shouldn't we go with you?" The short office asked.

"No, this jackass is all mine," Jody mumbled. Jody took off running to where she had last seen Vaughn. There was a rifle shot followed by three small arms shot. "Wade," Jody screamed as she got close to where the shots had been fired.

"Over here," Vaughn called out. Vaughn was seated at the base of the tree where he had hit the ground. "The shooter is over there. He shot at me, but I tripped on these hillbilly boots, and the shot went over my head. Then I capped his ass."

"God, what am I going to do with you?"

Winded, the lanky Patrolman ran up to Jody, who was helping Vaughn up. "We got cuffs but no suspect. This being a ghost town, are you sure you didn't arrest a ghost?"

"Slippery son of a bitch." Vaughn mumble.

Chapter Twenty-Two: Bryce on Ice

Two large guards led Bryce into an interview room. There were several steel tables with inmates chained at each table and the visitors seated on the opposite side. The tables were scatted to offer the illusion of privacy where none existed or was expected to. Guards patrolled between the tables and doled out angry stares to both prisoner and guest in a manner of territorial hierarchy. A small thing man sat down at the table Bryce was chained to. The man visiting Bryce wore a tailored suit and expensive cuff links. He was in his early to mid-thirties and looked like the poster boy for a prep school recruitment poster.

"Mr. Barrington, my name is Mr. Ironside. I will be your counsel of record."

Bryce had a black eye and a bruised face. Bryce's lip was swollen, and his right hand was wrapped in a bandage. Bryce continued to stare down at the table.

"Mr. Barrington, my name is Mr........"

"Fuck you." Bryce interrupted and stared up without lifting his head. "You think you are someone. What because you graduated at the top of your Ivy League class? Or because mommy and daddy have always given you just a little more than the neighbor's kids." Bryce paused and swallowed. "Then you come here and introduce yourself as Mister somebody. Fuck you."

After overhearing the second profanity, one of the guards smacked the back of Bryce's chair.

"What you are, my friend, is chattel. My family owns hundreds like you, and you are a fungible commodity. Easily eliminated or replaced. Where is the devil?"

"What?"

"Do not continue to validate your ignorance. I have been beaten senseless twice. There are guys here that say the first chance they get; they are going to rape me and pimp me out. Surely this is hell, so where is the person responsible for me being here?"

"You mean your sister?"

Bryce's eyes looked like they might catch aflame at any moment. "Do not refer to that demon as my sister."

"As you may or may not know, visitors here must sign an agreement that anything said during conversation can be recorded. If recorded, Mrs. Vaughn feared you might say something that may hurt the family."

"Listen, you little dickweed, you are going to get me out of here. And I don't mean sometime in the near future; I mean now. These assholes are planning to send me somewhere they say makes this place look like an amusement park. I cannot even wrap my mind around that."

"Well, that could be quite tricky," Ironside stated in a shaky voice.

"You like tricks here is one for you. Do you know what my family does?"

"Your family is the principal holders in a holding company."

"Wrong. But good guess. My family manages conflict worldwide. Not in the sense that we stop it. Quite the opposite, we start it. We stir it up, or we redirect it."

Ironside was starting to look nervous. "This is some of the talk Mrs. Vaughn was afraid you might conjure."

"Conjure. I like the word. Let me use it in a sentence. If you bastards don't get me the fuck out of here, I am going to conjure up a bunch of F.B.I., C.I.A., and maybe even the fucking P.T.A., and I am going to sing my ass off. You see, you shitheads have put me in a place where I have nothing to lose. I am not planning to spend the next twenty years as the pin-up girl for the Mississippi Department of Corrections."

A guard wandered by and hit Bryce's chair. "Sir, you have been warned before. This is your second warning."

"Sir, I suggest you rethink that statement," Ironside muttered.

"And I suggest you get the fuck out of here and start earning your worth."

Bryce looked at the guard who was coming to tell him he had to leave, but Bryce had said all he planned to say and held up his hands for the guard to lead him back to his cell.

Chapter Twenty-Three: A Day Off at Last

Lieutenant Singleton wore a clinging wrap-front midnight blue dress highlighting her curry form. She wore a gold necklace that dipped into her ample breasts, which were shamelessly exposed. Singleton had called Jody and Vaughn to an interview room at the Lamont Police station.

"Did my invite to the ball get lost in the mail?" Jody asked, eyeing Singleton.

"Don't be ridiculous; there is no ball. There is nothing wrong with a woman wanting to put on something other than her usual work clothes from time to time. What do you think, Detective Vaughn."

"I think you have exceptionally good taste."

"Why are we here? We have a case that is as hot as it can get," Jody asked.

"Yes, I know. I want you to file your report and take the rest of the day off."

"Are we suspended?"

"Oh. No, nothing like that. I never used that word. I had a talk with my boss down in Jackson. He used words like body count. And seemed to wonder why so many people seem to die when you are supposed to be off but are not."

"I can explain." Jody started.

"Yes, Detective Tyler and you usually do, but there is no need. Why don't you check in with your team or the team coach? And Detective

Vaughn, why don't you spend some quality time with your daughter? We can give the medical examiner a chance to catch up."

Jody wanted to laugh but did not dare.

"Detective Vaughn, you are excused. If you don't mind, Detective Tyler and I have a little girl talk to discuss."

Detective Vaughn stood and walked out of the room without another word.

"I know this is not professional, but I have got to ask you a question." Singleton started as soon as the door was closed.

Jody braced herself for the worst.

"Has he said anything about me?" Singleton looked at the door when Detective Vaughn had exited with the look of a lovesick schoolgirl.

"To be honest, ma'am no. He has not confided in me. He seems worried about his daughter. And he seems locked in a struggle with his soon-to-be ex-wife."

Singleton looked embarrassed for asking. "Why do so many smart, handsome men pick manipulative women?"

Jody knew she had reached her upper limit for diplomacy and just wanted out of the room. "Well, I will keep it confidential that you asked, and if he asks about you, I will let you know."

"Thank you." Singleton offered with the echo of desperation vibrating in her voice.

"WHAT WAS THAT ALL ABOUT?" Vaughn asked when Jody returned and started to finish the projects she had been working on.

"Minor problems."

"Anything I can help him with?"

"Yeah, but I really hope you don't."

Before Jody could leave, they had one last task. Jody and Vaughn made a call using the phone intercom so they could both be involved.

"Detective Lavon Tyler's desk, Abby Blackwell speaking." A woman's voice answered.

"Please put Detective Tyler on the phone," Jody instructed.

"Sorry, he is away from his desk. He is probably lurking around wherever they keep the dead bodies here in the new building. May I tell him who called?"

"Detective Tyler," Jody responded.

"Right. Like I said, he is not available."

"No, try and focus. My name is Detective Tyler."

"What happens to your voice? You sound so much more manly."

"You mean to tell me you are the idiot watching my brother's back."

"Sticks and stones. Now I am going to hang up now." Abby informed.

"Wait. Detective Blackwell, my name is Detective Wade Vaughn. You can check your I.D. registry and find me as a New York Detective. I have been relocated to Mississippi, and you will find me in the database there as well. I am willing to wait."

It took a moment for Abby to return to the phone. "Alright, detective, I show you listed. How can I help?"

"We have an open homicide. And we are trying to determine if there is an existing warrant or any other legal action pending on a Shavon Crabtree."

"Oh God, you guys have Calamity Jane? Is it possible for you to keep her out of my state?"

"We don't have her, but we think she is a witness or accomplice in the murders. Why do you refer to her as Calamity Jane."

"Because everywhere she goes, there is a disaster, and she usually walks away with only a few minor scratches. My system is telling me she has full release from all warrants. She has paid fines and court costs. Pretty good, considering she was trying to get an unconscious boy to sign paperwork so she could keep her trailer the last time I saw her."

"Thank you, Detective Blackwell. You have been a great help to our case," Vaughn informed Abby.

"And Abby, we are going to meet soon to have a little chat about your professionalism," Jody added.

"Can't wait." Abby disconnected.

Chapter Twenty-Four: Wendy the Shrink

Jody grabbed bottled beer and spent the evening with Wendy in Wendy's apartment, reviewing what they needed to do to prepare for the conference softball game. Wendy had searched the internet and found a video of the rival team, the Typhons. The Typhons were a great team and had often played their way through adversity.

"I need you to be sure to talk to the girls about the rule differences and to be sure they let their families know we are playing by conference rules, and some things they see may not be the same as what they are used to," Jody informed Wendy as she rested her eyes and took a long drink from her beer.

"Roger that."

"How do the girls feel about the game?"

"Are you kidding? They are pumped?"

"There is a good chance we are going to lose."

"Most likely. But when has that ever been the point?" Wendy opened another beer and took a deep swallow.

Jody began telling Wendy about her conversation with Singleton.

"So, your boss has got it bad for your new partner, and he doesn't have the slightest notion. So typical of the male of the species."

"You're making jokes. I have never felt so bad for someone I don't even like in all my life."

"In that case, it means I get to drink more beer while discussing it. I will play the role of your shrink."

"Thanks, that's what I need." Jody laid back on the couch, and Wendy continued to take drinks from her beer. "First question. Are you and Singleton best buddies?"

"No."

"Is there any reason for her to think you are?"

"No."

"Then don't most people have someone whose couch they plop down on and bare their souls to in times of crisis?"

"I would suppose."

"Then that means that she annoys you and everyone around her. That is why she has to go to her enemies. She is not capable of making friends."

"But it is all so sad." Jody sat up and drank more beer, trying to catch up with Wendy's level of intoxication.

"Alright, one last effort. Let us say Detective Vaughn's Frankenstein of a Wife signs over the divorce papers tomorrow. He is free to find a girlfriend. Someone who will not only be in his life for the long run but also in Sabrina's. Who do you think is a better candidate? You are the work-stealing boss of yours?"

Jody thought for a moment. "I have a question for you, Wendy."

"Shoot." Wendy slurred.

"Why are you wasting your time on the Board of Probation and Parole? You should be a physicist and making the big bucks."

"True, but then what would you and our gang of moppets do to stay out of trouble?"

THE FOLLOWING DAY, an F.B.I. agent, Waldron Clarkson, came to the Mississippi County Jail to interview Bryce. When Clarkson was led to Bryce's cell, Bryce was swinging by his throat. Dead to the world. Bryce had requested the interview, but it was not to be.

"What are you thinking?" The jailor asked Clarkson.

"I was thinking, I hope the peanuts on the flight back are not as stale as the ones coming here."

THE NEXT FEW DAYS WERE full of events for Jody and Vaughn. When not filling out paperwork for the multiple crimes committed, they followed up on leads, trying not to locate Darius, Shavon, and Marcus. Jody and Vaughn attended a memorial service for Tasha, a funeral for the slain officer from the motel, and a memorial service for Ricky Sells.

The Mississippi State trooper, police, and local sheriff were assisting in the search for Darius, but he had not been located so far. Jody secretly hoped other law enforcement officers would find Darius regardless of the outcome.

Marcus Newport and Shavon Crabtree had both seemed to vanish into thin air.

Chapter Twenty-Five: The Bobcats versus The Typhons

The day of the game had come, and it was different from the beginning of any game the Bobcats had played. They were a cable T.V. station that had chosen to air the game. News people who follow the Governor around were buzzing about. Even though the Typhon girls were approximately the same age as the Bobcats, the Typhons looked older and more mature.

"God, those look like full-grown-ass women," Robbie, the First Base girl, said when she saw the opposition lining up.

"That's what happens when you eat three meals a day, every day." Rosie, the catcher, commented. "I got to tell my mom and dad about this shit."

"Alright, ladies, cut the cussing. The ref can pull you from the game for that. Focus, and let's let them see what it is like to tussle with a Bobcat," Wendy instructed.

As ceremony dictated, the pitcher from the Typhons walked out to the mound, and Gloria, the Bobcat starting pitcher, met her for a handshake. The Governor, escorted by the head ref and a man carrying a radio microphone, also walked out to the mound.

"Ladies, let's have a clean game. And more importantly, let's have some fun," the head ref instructed. Governor, do you have any words you would like to share with both teams?"

The Governor leaned into the microphone. "One of the truest measures of our social evolutionary progress is through our past times. Today's game is an integral piece in making us better as people. As you watch the game, try not to miss the message it sends about the social healing of differences."

"We have a request." The Typhon pitcher stated.

"What is it?" The ref asked.

"That the governor throws out the first pitch would mean a lot to the conference and us."

"I would be honored." The Governor stated.

The two pitchers shook hands and prepared for the event to begin.

AS THE VISITING TEAM, Gloria pitched the first pitch. Typhon number 18 swung the bat on the first pitch, and there was a resounding crack that echoed through the college stadium. The ball launched like a rocket, shooting out of the stadium like a space shuttle liftoff.

Wendy turned to Jody and Vaughn and laughed. "This is going to be a dogfight."

"Heaven help my poor babies." Jody joked.

DURING THE FOURTH INNING, Marnice, the center fielder, executed a magnificent diving pop-fly catch. The only problem was that Marnice injured her wrist during the catch. Marnice wanted to continue to play, but Wendy knew this was not a good idea. Bertha was designated as the official utility and specialty replacement. Wendy knew, however, that, unlike the other teams the Bobcats had played, the Typhons were experts in running up the pitch count. This means they had derived techniques to deliberately tire the pitcher out so the pitcher would make a mistake. Wendy watched this on the videos she watched with Jody. Wendy decided to put her left fielder in for the right fielder in the center and to put Sabrina in the right field.

The problem came in the way of the next Typhon batter. The girl was left-handed. This meant that any pop fly ball this left-handed Typhon batter made would be coming straight for Sabrina. Another substitution would have worked, but the game rules required that at least one batter pass before an additional substitution was allowed.

The ball count went to 3 balls and two strikes, a full count. Wendy thought maybe I dodged a bullet. One more strike and the lefty could take a seat, and the game could proceed. But as frequently is the gift of what seemed the simple outcome was not to be. The lefty swung the bat at the next pitch, and there was a resounding crack as the ball connected with the bat. The ball blasted out as if propelled by a cannon, a waist-high line drive past Robie, the first baseman. The ball hit the ground, took out a divot, and ricocheted toward the right field. Sabrina charged the ball and caught it before it had barely cleared its hop. Sabrina slid in the dirt as her legs seemed to get the change direction command a tenth of a second later than the rest of her body. Sabrina fired the ball on a spin move and sent the ball a light speed to first base. The snap of the ball hitting the Robie's glove made the entire crowd take a collective gasp. Lefty was out. Sabrina brushed herself off and headed back to her waiting position.

DESPITE THE AUSPICIOUS start of the Typhons, the game was closely matched, so much so that by the seventh inning strength, the score was tied 10 to 10. The crowed exuberated energy and all had been sucked into a game the was greater than any could expect.

Wendy stood with Vaughn, Jody, and Felix walked up. "Excuse me, Detective Tyler. Would it be inappropriate if I asked you out?"

The small group stood and stared at Jody. "No, Sir. I would not find that inappropriate; however, I have to respectfully decline because I have other plans." Jody winked at Wendy.

Wendy then stated. "Felix, would you find it inappropriate if I asked you out? My treat and I pick the place?"

Felix seemed to struggle to put together the appropriate sounds to make words.

"I take that to be a confirmation, so write down your number, and I will make arrangements," Wendy instructed. "Now, if you will excuse me, I must get my team fired up."

Sabrina ran up to Vaughn and grabbed his arm. Sabrina pointed, and there was Marcus Newport and the man, another man who had escaped the shooting at the Tucker bar, walking toward Jody and Vaughn.

"And me without my shotgun," Jody stated.

"Relax, he is not here for a gunfight," Vaughn informed.

"How do you know?"

"Because it is daylight, and we can see him."

"Nice to see the both of you again." Marcus smiled.

"I should arrest you." Jody sneered at Marcus.

"No need to cause a scene, Detective Tyler. I only came to deliver a message."

"What is the message, Marcus?" Vaughn asked.

"Your wife requests a few moments of your time privately to discuss some personal matters."

"I'll be right back. Take Sabrina to the pep talk." Vaughn instructed.

"How can boys be so darn cavalier about stuff like that." To Sabrina, who gave Jody a reassuring hug.

"GET IN AND CLOSE THAT damn door," Viola stated. Marcus has led Vaughn to a limo parked at the back of the ballpark parking lot.

"How long have you been here?" Vaughn asked, getting into the limo.

"Long enough to see a girl that should be training to be the leader of the free world rolling around in the dirt." Viola paused and visually admired her husband for the moment." You know it is supposed to be spring, but this pace is over 80 with 100-degree humidity." Viola stared at Vaughn for a moment, sizing him up.

"Sorry to hear about Bryce."

"No, you are not. You never like him, and he never like you."

"Still a terrible way to end it all."

"So, you don't think my father had something to do with it?"

"Doesn't matter. I have enough innocent people to protect. The Bryce's of the word is an antidotal footnote on a police file."

They stared for a moment. "I love you. I want you to know that. I want you to come home, but maybe that is just not going to happen. I need to cut my losses before things go any further awry."

Vaughn was seated in the limo across from his wife. He took her hand. "I know you do, and that is what complicates things so much."

"Do you love this muscle woman?" Viola asked.

"Our problem is not about her. I did not know her when I left. The problem we have deals with me and you and Sabrina."

"I did not mean to make her hate me." Viola confessed.

"Time will help her heal."

"I will sign the papers, but I have conditions."

"What conditions?"

"First, you will volunteer no information on anything you learned about my family business. That means that unless you are contacted by a government agency with a written request, you will not disclose anything detrimental to my family business."

"Vi, I don't want to hurt you. I just want you to know your daughter is not defective. She is a loving human being. I agree."

"Settled. Next condition. I want another baby."

"I think that one deserves a little more clarity."

"All my fathers' brothers have sons. My father is afraid that, at some point, we will be weeded out of the company business. So, you give me another child, and you keep Sabrina. And I sign the papers making you a free man."

"This is not moral in the least."

"The way I see it, you have your choice. We can do it artificial insemination. You can help me pick a surrogate womb. Can we do it the old-fashioned way with a bottle of wind and some soothing music?"

"How long do I get to decide?"

"Decide now, and so I don't ever have to come back to this God-forsaken state, and I will tell you where you can find Darius Youngblood."

Vaughn made his decision and kissed his wife before leaving the limo. It was a devil's deal, but it was the only deal on the table.

"I SEE THINGS WENT WELL," Jody stated as Vaughn returned, and the Bobcats were preparing to restart the game.

"What makes you say that?" Vaughn asked. Wendy picked up a towel and walked over to wipe the lipstick smear from Vaughn's mouth. "Not your shade, Detective."

"We are going to miss the end of the game. I know where Darius is, and we have to go now." Vaughn stated.

"IT WAS A KISS TO SEAL an agreement," Vaughn said as he and Jody sped toward the Rex Foxx Inn. Jody had borrowed a police pick-up while her car was being repaired for gunshots.

"I would never ask a married man why he kisses his wife." Jody snapped.

"For Pete's sake, Jody, don't you see this is why I wanted to wait until the papers for my divorce were in hand? I don't want to hurt you or have you feel compromised. I need your trust. I despise the Darius of the world. They make every chance at a relationship with someone you meet and care about an inquisition. I am no saint but sometimes even a saint can fail an inquisition."

"I trust you. But it doesn't mean I have to like it."

"She will sign the papers tomorrow and air mail them, but there are a couple of conditions."

Vaughn explained the terms, and Jody did not like them.

JODY AMBLED UP THE frame outdoor stairs to the motel, following Vaughn. Technically, she should have been in the lead because she was clearly the lead detective, but she did not want to challenge Vaughn for it.

"Sir, there is a problem with your payment," Vaughn said, banging on the door. The door opened, and there was Shavon naked, holding a towel in front of herself. From the doorway, they could see Darius wearing only his boxers, lying on the bed. Jody gave Shavon a look that caused her to shiver more than being undressed. Jody grabbed Shavon, and Vaughn grabbed Jody's arm to keep her focused on the arrest at hand. Jody ended up with the towel in her hand as the naked Shavon ran from the room.

"Three holes alright. Positive identification." Vaughn stated.

"Hey babe, I am glad you are here. The new boyfriend is really a contract killer. He is here for my action."

"Get up, Darius Youngblood; you are under arrest," Jody announced.

"Jody, you have known me all your life. This guy just hit town. He aint one of us."

Jody holstered her weapon and removed her handcuffs. "Stand up, please."

Darius started to get out of the bed, then grabbed a pistol from beneath the pillow and shot Vaughn, who still had his gun pointed toward Darius. Vaughn fell backward, hit the wall, and then sank to the floor.

"Oh, shit, what did you just do?" Jody screamed.

"He came to kill me, and you led him right here to me."

"Shoot him, Jody," Vaughn called out in a faint voice.

"See, he is hell-bent on executing me."

"Jody, they were shooting at you the night at the ghost town. Those are the same guys Dela saw throw the firebomb in his mother's old house. They were working for him."

Jody looked at Darius, now seeing him differently than she had ever had.

"Those tree stands they were shooting from had to have up in the trees long before we got there." Vaughn further explained.

Tears started filling Jody's eyes as she saw her youth mistakes marching before her.

"I need to finish off this lying piece of shit city boy. He is poisoning your mind."

"He has to kill you. Don't worry about me. Around his neck is a plastic handcuff key on a leather tie. It is an old dope dealer's trick. He was planning to kill you and leave your body in that ghost town." Vaughn's voice seemed to trail off.

Jody noticed the gun was still in Darius's hand. Slowly, Darius started to aim the weapon at Vaughn again. "Please drop the gun, Darius. I am begging you one last time."

Darius took his bead on Vaughn, and Jody drew her .45 semi-automatic 1911 and shot Darius multiple times. The rounds from Jody's .45 passed through Darius, leaving him with a look of amazement on his face. Jody dived to the floor and grabbed Vaughn.

Vaughn's eyes looked weak from blood loss. "Hey Jody. Remember that night you kissed me, and you said the thing that scared you the most is that I might push you away or that I might not kiss you back."

"Save your strength. I already have a little girl to answer to."

"I was scared you would run to him before you ran to me."

"Keep that in mind when you decide on your sperm delivery method for your wife. If it is up to me, you can mix it in a mason jar and mail it."

THE FINAL SCORE FOR the softball game was 18 to 17. The Typhons won mathematically, but there was a big victory for the Bobcats because they proved they could hold their own against a conference team. Several conference coaches watched the game and wondered why some of the Bobcat girls were not playing in a real conference league game.

Chapter Twenty-Six: Invitation to a Wedding.

"You got him shot?" Singleton asked, out of breath, as she rushed into the Lamont fire station. Singleton wore a low-cut tangerine dress and matching leather shoes. It was clear she had been searching for Jody.

"No. I didn't get him shot." Jody responded, standing in the firehouse looking at the fire pole that went through a hole in the ceiling.

"Then he was not shot?" Singleton tried to clarify.

"Yes, he was shot."

"I thought you just said you did not get him shot."

"I did."

"I hate circular conversations. Is he in the hospital or not?'

"Yes, Detective Vaughn is in the hospital," Jody answered. "The doctors say the bullet rode along his rib. He has a couple of fractured ribs. There was quite a bit of blood loss, but he is going to be alright."

At that moment, Sabrina rode down the fire pole.

"Is this his daughter?" Singleton whispered.

"Yes, and you don't have to whisper. She knows she's his daughter and she even if she didn't, she can't hear you."

"Well, I thought I would go and see him."

"That explains the dress."

"Too much?"

"He told me that he has finally got his wife to sign the divorce papers. His wife, now ex-wife, is a powerful woman in the business sector."

"So."

"So, a powerful woman in a position of authority may be a little frightening to him right now. You may be ruining an opportunity for a future relationship."

Sabrina stared for a moment as if nothing she was detecting made sense to her, then ran for the stairs for another ride on the pole.

"If that is your way of saying, take it easy on your partner so you don't lose him. I will let you know. I think having Detective Vaughn as your partner is an excellent idea. Maybe he can keep you out of trouble." With this statement Singleton stated leaving.

"Let him know I will bring Sabrina by later." Jody requested.

"THE LADY FROM THE DEPARTMENT of Family Service found a school for Sabrina. Why didn't you tell me that people were having problems placing her because she is advanced for her age in most studies." Jody asked Vaughn as he lay in bed at the hospital.

"She likes being one of the gang when it comes to being a person that I could not take that away from her. She has had private tutors and special aids for all her life."

"Well, now she has Wendy. Because Wendy says that she can stay as part of the team as long as her schoolwork stays caught up."

Sabrina started signing something for her father and then left the room.

"What was that all about?" Jody asked.

"She says she is not a baby, and she knows we need to talk about us."

"Well, both of you are invited to my bother Lavon's wedding. Weddings in the Tyler family are always big family events, and the more young people, the better."

"Singleton will ask you if you think you need a different partner. She feels like I let you get shot."

"Darius shot me for the same reason he felt he had to shoot you. It is, by the way, the same reason you hesitated for a fraction of a second."

"What is that, my mental heavy-lifting partner?"

"You did not see yourself just killing Darius but also, for once and all severing most of your connections to the humps and bumps of adolescence."

"So, killing me would be like a right of ascension making him a full fledge gangster. What do you think happened to Marcus and his man?"

"I am sure he is in Hong Kong having a suit made by now. And if I measure it correctly Honk Kong is 8399 miles outside our jurisdiction. Marcus is a mercenary that works for Viola's family."

"Do I need to ask why her family needs mercenaries and why one seems to know you so well?"

"Jody, I have not lied to you. If we are going to work together, you must understand the agreement I made with my soon-to-be ex-wife: I don't get to discuss their business. That is the same agreement that will let me keep Sabrina safe."

"Does that mean you plan to keep me as a partner?"

"I would love to keep you as a partner, Jody Tyler. And for the record, you were right about one thing in particular."

"Do tell."

"Singleton was here apologizing about pressuring me to have a relationship with her. I had no idea that was on her mind. I thought she was dressing up for a possible T.V. interview."

"Well, you know what they say. The hot guy is always the last to know."

"Guys pressure women a little differently."

JODY SAT BY HERSELF in the lonely waiting area. It was the middle of the night, and it was past Sabrina's bedtime, when everything was supposed to be, but Jody could not bring herself not to allow Sabrina some time alone with her father. Jody knew there was no way for her to comprehend the rapid sign language she saw as she was leaving the room. Still, Jody knew Sabrina was telling her father about the parts of the game that he had missed and about locating a new school. Jody was equally sure Vaughn was busy telling he daughter that to keep her he had been forced to make certain compromises. Those compromises might include her someday having a brother or sister who might never want anything to do with Sabrina.

Jody searched the purse she had brought with her and found a ragged leather-bound bible. All the Tyler children had received a similar bible from their mother when they had decided it was time to venture out on their own. Their mother had told them they did not have to read it. But they had to take it wherever they were. As a gift from her it was like taking a part of her along with them.

"Momma it's me Jody" Jody had thumbed the bible for a moment then thought it was important to call her mother.

"Jody Diane Tyler, it may be the middle of the night, but a mother knows the sound of her own children. Where are you?" Rebecca Tyler asked in a sleepy haze.

"I am at the hospital in Starkville."

"Oh, baby, are you alright? Do you need me to come get you?"

"No, ma'am, I am fine. My new partner got shot during an arrest."

"I am sorry to hear that. Will he live?" Rebecca asked.

"Yes, ma'am."

There was a silence on the line, and both women knew the conversation was far from over.

"Momma, I had to terminate the threat." Jody began again.

There was another silence; this time, it was clear that Rebecca Tyler was carefully selecting the next words. "You have had to terminate a threat before. I have heard your father tell you guys that your partner's life is in your hands, and his life is in your hands. At some point, you may have to decide on the value of saving their life as it relates to risking or ending that of a suspect or your own."

"I know that momma. But the life I terminated was Darius Youngblood."

Now, the silence shared was all about a mother and daughter reliving the past.

"Momma, I called to say thank you. I know there may be some people shortly who will question my shoot. Some people may be harboring nasty things and waiting for a chance to speak to them. But before any of that starts, I want to say thank you to you and Dad."

"For what baby?"

"For putting up with me when I was a know-it-all teen. For not listening to you about compromising my virtues. Oh, momma, I am sorry for getting in an argument when you insisted, I end the affair with Darius."

"Baby, I am the mother to all of you guys, and no one of you has followed the exact path of the other. No one of you has been or will be perfect. But keep in mind that no matter what you do, I love you. Now I love you not only when you do what I say and what I want you to, but I love you for being you."

One last time there was a silence this one represented unity.

"Now I have got to get some sleep. Your father is driving Kim and me to Shepherds Pass in the morning. He snores like a busted chainsaw. I will be on minimum sleep. I must measure Lynn for her dress. And I need you to get there too, I don't want you bursting out of your clothes in the middle of the church reception. I didn't raise any strippers. Speaking of which, do you know who you are bringing for the dance?"

"Yes, momma."

"Good."

"Good night, momma."

"Good night, baby."

Though no quantifiable axiom would explain it, the world was starting to shift back into place for Jody Diane Tyler the bull in the China shop.

Also by Alex Mitchell

www.ingramcontent.com/pod-product-compliance
Lightning Source LLC
Chambersburg PA
CBHW020147180626
46810CB00004B/1767